# SAVE ME

JILL SANDERS

DIGITAL ISBN: 978-1-945100-57-4

PRINT ISBN: 979-8-826354-30-8

PRINT: 978-1-945100-63-5



Copyeditor: Erica Ellis – inkdeepediting.com

## SUMMARY

*"The police are not ruling out the possibility that they have discovered the lair of a serial killer..."*

It was the stuff of nightmares. Crissy had survived, but she was the only one out of a dozen women who could claim so. That didn't mean she had gotten away unscathed, physically or mentally. Being held prisoner for days and repeatedly beaten and raped hadn't been the end of it. Losing the one man she'd trusted to help her recover had been the final blow. Now, as a single parent, she's headed down the coast with her daughter to look for some peace of mind. Never in her wildest dreams did she imagine that trouble would follow her.

Brock could never forget that fateful night he'd found the broken woman in the locked container. The fear and gratefulness in her haunting blue eyes would stay with him forever. As would knowing that it had been his partner who had tortured her and a dozen more unfortunate souls. That knowledge left him wondering if he could ever trust anyone again. But when he found out that someone was threatening the blue-eyed beauty once more, he knew that he would have to do something drastic to save her and to mend what was broken in himself.

# PROLOGUE

Darkness.

For a split second, panic overtook her. But then the rhythmic hum of a motor and the gentle sway of the car had her body relaxing.

Just as she was about to sink back into the abyss, memories surfaced. Bodies rubbing against one another, bumping and grinding. Loud music piercing her ears, drowning out voices, until all that was left was the beat of the song pounding in her head. The bitter alcohol that had warmed her and dulled her mind earlier now soured her tongue and unsettled her stomach. Her vision was blocked by the false lashes that she normally wore to work. Now they were glued together by her thick mascara and sealed her eyes shut.

Why had she allowed Carl to talk her into working at the club again? It had only been ten months since she'd given birth.

Carl always complained that he'd wanted to be married to a stripper. Only Crissy didn't have what it took, upstairs at least, to dance on stage and make money. So she did what she'd been doing before she'd married him. What she'd done for all of her life, it seemed. She'd waited tables. She didn't mind where she worked, a diner or a strip club, just as long as the tips were good.

And they were good enough to keep her working at Sunset Strip, one of the hottest strip clubs along the Miami coast.

She'd changed her looks over the year that she'd worked there, dying her dark hair a bright blonde and wearing skintight outfits to fit in with the rest of the girls working tables and dancing on the stages.

But then she'd gotten pregnant and had believed that her long hours of wearing heels and getting felt up by creepy men was over. But two weeks after she'd had Emma, Carl had lost his job, and she'd had to go back to work at the club.

Carl had talked her into going back, saying it was "easy money." Easy for him, at least. The long hours, the sore feet and back, and having to constantly turn away unwanted advances wasn't something her husband thought about or even cared to hear about.

She'd hoped that Carl would find another job. After all, Miami was full of bartending jobs, the only thing that he'd ever been good at. Instead, he'd turned to the bottle, and she suspected that wasn't all.

To anyone looking from the outside, Carl had painted a picture of a caring husband and father. And at first, he had been. After losing his job, he'd slowly sunk lower and basically stopped trying. Oh, he still kept up the outward appearances to everyone they knew, but at home, he was different. He'd changed so much that she didn't even recognize him any longer.

Days turned into weeks, and he'd sunk further into a

darkness. She didn't have the time to help pull him out of the funk. Since they were behind on their bills, she'd taken a second job working behind a counter at a bakery a few doors down from their one-bedroom apartment. Which meant she worked from seven at night until eleven in the morning, seven days a week.

After coming home more than once to find him passed out and Emma crying, she'd had to start paying for a babysitter. She'd even worried that Carl wasn't feeding their daughter since she had started looking extremely underweight.

Of course, if she said anything, he would start an argument with her. He'd claim he'd been so busy that day trying to find work that he'd just needed one drink to soothe his nerves. Or he'd complain that with a crying kid hooked to him, there was no way he would be able to find work.

The fights with Carl filled up what precious time she had to herself or with Emma. Clinging to the baby, she'd listen while Carl explained his responsibilities away and laid them solely onto her shoulders.

After all, everything in life was Crissy's fault, in the eyes of Carl. She supposed she'd walked right into the abusive relationship. After suffering at the hands of her father for all of her childhood, she had clung to the first man who'd smiled at her and promised to take her far away from her father's fists.

Following up a physically abusive relationship with an emotionally abusive one had sucked out what little joy Crissy had left in life.

In the coming days, what she had to endure would take the rest of it until she was nothing more than a shell of a woman, determined to give her daughter everything she had never had. Happiness.

# CHAPTER ONE

Crissy stopped and took a moment to breathe in the salty warm air. One second, two, three... Then the phone rang, breaking through the soft sound of the wind rustling the palm fronds, the bees buzzing around the flowers that she had planted a few weeks earlier, and the sounds of the gulls crying as they flew far overhead.

She rushed back across the pathway, set the basket full of laundry down on the table, and answered the phone.

"Paradise Place, how may I help you?" she answered cheerfully.

The caller sounded like an older woman, and after answering her questions about the rental house and walking her through the steps to book the place online, Crissy picked up the laundry basket and headed back across the pool courtyard into the main rental property.

The home—Paradise Place—was a six-bedroom, seven-bath, four-thousand-square-foot beauty. There was a massive swimming pool and patio between the main home and the pool house. Thick tropical foliage filled every nook and cranny of the property, secluding the residence from the homes on either side.

The place was owned by the chief of police in Key West, who used the property as a year-round rental and income property. They rented it out on a monthly basis, as local laws excluded short-term rentals on Key West. The business was run and operated solely by hers truly.

After what had happened to her, Reggie Miller and his wife, Kimberly, had contacted her and convinced her to run the place. At the time the Millers had contacted her for the job, she hadn't had any other work opportunities. After an initial meeting with the couple, who lived on one of the other Keys, she and Emma had moved from Miami to Key West.

She'd needed work and a place to live, since Carl hadn't paid their rent on the small one-bedroom apartment once she'd been kidnapped.

She'd left the hospital almost three months after she'd arrived there broken and almost dead and had been surprised to find out that Carl had sold all of her belongings, even her clothes. He'd been renting a small hotel room in the bad part of Miami and expected her and Emma to live there with him. The first night, there'd been a shooting just outside their room. The second, someone had tried to break in. She and Emma hadn't stayed for a third night.

Instead, she'd talked her friends Emily and Rafe into letting her and Emma stay with them until she could get back on her feet. Less than a month later, she'd filed for divorce from Carl.

She and Emma had fit nicely into the smaller two-and-a-half-bedroom pool house that sat on the back of the large rental property in Key West. The half bedroom was actually a large loft, which Emma had moved into shortly after her second birthday. She'd turned the space into a perfect little girl's bedroom and play area.

Living in paradise, being self-reliant, and not having to wait tables and be around strangers all day was good for her recovery. Most importantly, it was good for Emma.

Carl's absence from their lives was only a good thing. It allowed her and her daughter to blossom and heal. She'd won sole custody after Carl had shown up to divorce court high and raging about how this was eating into his online gaming time. The female judge had closed the case quickly, assuring her that Emma wouldn't have to spend an hour of her life with Carl and that she wouldn't have to pay him any alimony, which he'd screamed in court was his due.

After that day, she hadn't seen or heard from Carl once. They were better off for it, but it still stung. She'd thought Carl was the one.

He'd saved her from the horrors of her childhood. She had never had to worry that Carl would lift a fist to her. He may have yelled and been a basic child in a lot of areas, but he'd never hit her.

Back then, she'd believed she needed to be with someone. That she needed a man to save her from... well, a worse man.

Now, she no longer cared if she grew old by herself, just as long as Emma was happy. And thankfully, her daughter was flourishing.

How was it that Emma was almost three already? Crissy stilled as she thought back to the joy of holding her daughter for the first time.

Other memories filled her mind as well.

The first year after... what had happened to her, everything was a blur. She'd spent months in the hospital and then even longer in recovery, learning simple things like how to walk and how to hold a fork again. Thanks to Emily, she hadn't had to worry about Emma during that time. Her friends Emily and Jamie had stepped up and saw to her daughter's every need while Crissy recovered.

After all, the two women had almost gone through what she had. It was because of them, and their now husbands Rafe and Blaine, that Crissy was alive today.

She'd gone to a counselor almost daily, learning to breathe through the panic attacks, just trying to live again. Even now, she walked three blocks to the small office for weekly meetings with Dr. Elizabeth Rizzo.

The psychologist wanted to meet with Emma as well, but Crissy was determined to keep every aspect of her dark past away from her daughter. Besides, Emma was just two months shy of her third birthday. She didn't even remember Crissy struggling to learn how to walk or being broken and bandaged up any longer.

Shaking any thoughts of her past away, she got back to the task at hand—making the beds, cleaning the bathrooms, replacing any soiled towels with fresh ones, emptying the trash cans, and removing any food or items left in the rental. Once she was sure everything was perfect, she sent a text message off to the new renters, telling them that the property was ready for check-in. She received an almost immediate response that they were en route. ETA thirty minutes.

That gave her half an hour to herself. She stepped out onto the patio and scooped some leaves out of the large lagoon pool and added a bag of salt to the water. She enjoyed maintaining the pool and found it extremely calming. Then she peeled off her tank top and shorts and dove into the refreshing crystal-clear water.

Taking these small moments to herself, as the doctor suggested, was something she had to force herself to do. If it were up to Crissy, she'd fill each waking moment with work or time with her daughter. She couldn't really afford to let her mind wander. Not when it kept whizzing her back to the shipping container where she'd been held.

Since her mind wouldn't stop that train of thought as she floated, looking up at the cloudless blue sky, she flipped over and did a few laps until she was breathless. With each stroke, she focused only on her breathing and the sound of her heartbeat.

When her phone chimed that there was someone at the front gate, she climbed out, shook the water from her short hair, pulled on her clothes, and went to greet the new guests.

This month's renters were a large family—three siblings and their four young kids under ten, along with their parents. The large group would fill the house to capacity. The closeness of the family and the ease with which everyone interacted made her jealousy surface, as it always did.

In the past year that she'd worked there, she'd seen it all. Families that constantly fought with one another, ones that ignored each other, and ones that truly loved one another. This seemed to be the latter. And as much as it hurt her to see, she was thankful for it.

The other types of families were a drain on her and sometimes the house. In the past year, she'd had to learn how to repair drywall after one particularly violent fight between a father and his son.

After getting everyone settled, she walked next door to gather Emma from her morning play session with her neighbor Beth and her three-in-a-half-year-old daughter Tilly.

Beth was a stay-at-home mother whom Crissy had

instantly liked. She trusted her with Emma completely. Emma and Tilly had become best friends days after they'd moved there.

Beth's husband was owner and head chef at one of Key West's most expensive restaurants, Oliver's, which had been named after him by his parents when they'd started the place back when he'd been a child.

Crissy opened the back screen door on the smaller home and stepped into the kitchen without knocking.

Beth was sitting at the table, feeding her one-year-old, Johnathan, while Emma and Tilly sat on the floor across the living space, watching cartoons.

"So?" Beth asked. "Did the group get settled?"

"Yes." Crissy sat down with a sigh. "It's a larger group this time. A nice family with kids. I think they'll be fairly quiet for the month."

"Good." Beth sighed. "The last group kept Oliver up."

"Yeah, it's hard to gauge just how crazy groups of retirees are going to get."

"Who knew that a bunch of eighty-year-olds could party that hard." Beth laughed.

"Hey, when I'm that old, I want to have friends like that I can party with," Crissy joked.

"Ditto." Beth smiled as she wiped her son's face. "I can watch her longer today, if you want to take some time?"

Crissy started to deny Beth, but then shrugged. "I have been meaning to walk to the store. We're low on a few things." Her eyes moved to Emma, who hadn't even acknowledged her presence yet. "If you're sure?"

"Totally. Besides, they're really into the cartoons." Beth motioned towards the two girls.

Standing up, Crissy nodded. "I'll be back in half an hour."

"Take your time," Beth said, waving her away.

She stepped back through the gate into her own yard and grabbed the little red wagon she and Emma used to wheel groceries from the little store two blocks away.

The two-block walk to the store was one of her small joys in life. Just knowing she could walk anywhere on her own without fear thrilled her. Her body had almost returned to normal and as she waved to all of the locals along the path, she felt safe.

The part of town the house was in wasn't full of rentals like a lot of areas in the Keys. Most of the homes around it were smaller and older and owned by longtime locals. The pool house was actually the original residence on the land and sat at the front of a small cul-de-sac street. The lot filled the space between two streets and the newer, larger home sat at the front of the property along a main thoroughfare. The pool was directly in the middle of the two structures. The bigger place and the pool had been built fewer than five years ago.

Leaving her cart outside, Crissy stepped into the store and started gathering the needed items in a basket. She was in the bread aisle when she heard the news report from the television that sat over the cashier.

"Today marks the two-year anniversary since the second of the Miami serial-killer brothers was unmasked. Days after Scott Alcott's body was discovered in a car at the bottom of a lake, Alcott's half-brother Daryl Collins, a Miami police officer and Alcott's partner in crime, was shot and killed during a kidnapping gone wrong. Collins's last victim…"

A loud ringing blocked the rest of the news report. How had she forgotten today was the anniversary? How had she missed such an important date?

The panic attack had her doubled over. Her fingers dug into the loaf of bread that she'd just grabbed off the shelf to place in her basket.

Breathe, she told herself several times. But the report continued to circle in her head. Two years. It had been two years since she'd been rescued from hell.

This was the reason she didn't own a television. This was why Emma had to go next door to watch cartoons. She wanted to forget. To let those anniversaries go by without remembering...

Breathe-one, breathe-two, breathe-three. She counted until the buzzing in her head stopped and her vision corrected.

She set down her basket of items and rushed towards the door. She stood outside gulping fresh sea air until she felt sure the report had ended. When she stepped back inside, the owner of the store looked at her funny as she walked over and picked up her basket.

Not giving the woman any reasons for her behavior, she continued shopping and even added a fake smile on her lips as she moved around the store.

"Are you okay, miss?" the woman asked when she rang up her items.

"Yes, I suppose I just got overheated on the walk here." She quickly changed the subject.

The walk home wasn't as enjoyable as the walk there, but still, it gave her plenty of time to settle herself before seeing her daughter.

She even took the extra time to put all of the groceries away before collecting Emma. The large family was out enjoying the pool when she and Emma stepped back into the yard.

She held Emma in her arms, her daughter instantly happy upon seeing the kids splashing in the pool.

"Pool, Mama." Emma clapped.

"Not right now, honey. Lunch and nap first." She shifted to open the door just as the phone rang again.

Putting her daughter down, she answered the call with her standard greeting, smiling and ready to answer any questions about the rental.

"You think you got off scot-free?" the deep voice hissed. "You'll pay for escaping us."

Shortly after the phone clicked, Crissy's vision grayed, and she slid to the floor and landed on the tile with a thud.

<h1 style="text-align:center">CHAPTER TWO</h1>

Before his cell phone disconnected, Brock was heading outside towards his car.

It had been two years. Two long years filled with guilt and shame. Time he'd spent trying to make up for being so blind.

Knowing that he'd allowed his partner to do those horrible things right under his nose had weighed so heavily on him that it had almost cost him everything.

The day after finding the broken blue-eyed woman in the shipping container, where his partner Daryl Collins had spent years raping and murdering women, he'd handed in his badge.

Thankfully, his captain had shoved it back at him and put him on desk duty. He'd spent the next few months seeing a shirk. It had helped. A little.

The weight of the guilt was something he didn't think he could ever overcome. Ever.

He'd done everything he could think of to rectify his oversight. Except one. Apologize to the ones that had been hurt by his blindness and stupidity.

He knew right where Crissy and her daughter Emma where. Hell, it was because of his guilt that they were in Key West in the first place.

"Where are you heading?" Joe, his current chief, asked as he walked towards the front door of the station.

"I just got a call from my folks," Brock said, stopping just inside the door. "I need some personal time," he said, not wanting to go into the details.

Joe nodded without even asking. "How much personal time?"

Brock jerked in a breath. Hell. What was he doing? His dad had mentioned that Crissy had called him and told him she'd received a threatening call, and the first thought he had was to go running down to the Keys. To do what? Reach through the phone and kick whatever sicko had found out where she lived and decided to mess with her? Taking a deep breath, Joe waited.

"Wanna come into my office and have a chat?" Joe suggested when Brock didn't answer.

Since he didn't have any reason not to, Brock followed him back down the hallway and sat in the chair across from Joe's desk.

"Before Reggie called you, he called me," Joe started. He held up his hand to stop Brock from saying anything. "Our friendship goes back long before you ever came along," Joe joked. "Which is why I knew for sure that you'd be heading toward the door." Joe watched him.

"Yeah." Brock relaxed back in the chair.

"Which is why your father and I have decided you might need a change of scenery," Joe said. Brock leaned forward again.

"Joe, I don't want—"

"I don't give a rat's butt what you want. I'm here to give

you what you need. And right now, your father needs someone with your skills down there."

Hadn't he just wanted that? Why then was his first thought to decline the offer? Unsure of why, he sat in silence instead.

Joe tilted his head and continued. "It'll be for a month at first. Then we'll play it by ear. I'm leaving it up to Reggie's discretion as to how long this assignment will last." Joe held out his hand. "Turn in your badge and weapon. You'll get new ones down there. Your dad is waiting."

Something close to anger bubbled in Brock's chest at being manipulated again, but then the memory of Crissy's blue eyes looking up at him resurfaced. He'd never forget seeing her chained like an animal to the floor of the shipping container, covered in dirt and blood. The guilt had him standing and handing over his badge and sidearm.

Joe secured both items in the locked cabinet behind his desk. Then he held out his hand for Brock's. "I've always known I had you temporarily. Your dad's been trying to convince me to transfer you down there for years."

"He has?" Brock asked as he shook the man's hand.

Joe leaned closer and joked, "My guess is he's wanting to retire soon and wants you to fill the spot."

That was news to Brock. His father had been chief of police in Key West since... well, as long as Brock could remember. It was because of his dad that Brock had gone into the force in the first place.

After graduating from the academy, Brock had chosen to stay in Miami instead of heading back home. He hadn't wanted any special attention because he was the chief's son. Also, he'd liked being where the action was. Or so he'd thought.

"Thanks," Brock said to Joe.

"If I'm lucky, I'll have you back in no time," Joe added. "Good luck down there. Even if you don't believe me, you deserve the break," he added with a nod.

"Right," Brock answered. He swallowed the lump in his throat.

It took him a few moments to gather up his personal items and say a few goodbyes. It took him longer to pack up a bag and get Chester into his carrying case. The massive black cat had become his support animal shortly after finding out about Daryl.

He'd taken the drive to the Keys many times over the years and, before he knew it, he was on Highway One, stuck in all the tourist traffic. His parents' home was on Shark Key, one of the most secure, exclusive, and expensive Keys. The home had been in the family long before he'd been born.

His parents had done updates any time a storm ripped the roof or deck off, but not much more. The property, which was easily worth four million in today's market, could use a little more updating, in his opinion.

After passing through the security gate and having a chat with one of the guards on duty, he headed to the very tip of the Key.

He parked his Jeep behind his father's patrol car, grabbed his bags and Chester's carrying case, and headed up the front steps.

Setting his bag down just inside the glass double front doors, he called out, "Mom? Dad?"

"Back here," his mother answered almost immediately. They would have known he was coming, as the security gate always notified the residents when a visitor passed through.

Taking Chester with him, he headed further inside. He

hadn't expected his parents to have company and stilled just inside the living area. Seeing Crissy Talbot sitting on his parents' sofa, holding her daughter, shocked him. He hadn't been prepared to see her again just yet.

The last time he'd seen her, she'd been broken, bleeding, and half dead. Now, she was healed, tan, and very healthy looking.

The matted bleached blonde hair she'd had back then was gone, replaced with a darker pixie cut that somehow made her appear healthier and very appealing. She was tiny.

She sat in faded jean shorts, an oversized T-shirt, and worn flip flops. She could easily have been a tourist in the Keys.

If not for the fear hidden behind those piercing blue eyes of hers, he could have easily mistaken her for someone else.

"Here he is now," his father said, standing up and walking over to wrap his arms around him.

Brock set Chester's container down and easily wrapped his arms around his father, never once taking his eyes from Crissy's.

"What's all this?" he asked quietly.

"This," his father said, standing back, "is your new assignment."

He hadn't expected his father to be so up front with the woman. Or with him, for that matter. When he'd talked to his dad on the trip down there, his father hadn't once mentioned that Crissy knew he would be watching out for her and her daughter.

His father had made it seem like he'd be joining the Key West force and working the standard beat.

"Okay," Brock said, wrapping his arms around his mother, who had followed his dad over for a hug.

It had been a few months since he'd last seen them, but no matter the time between the visits, their greetings were always the same. They greeted him like a son who had been away for years, and somehow that always cheered him up, knowing that they loved him that much. Few of his friends growing up had been lucky enough to have parents who had stuck together or even cared in the least about their children.

His dad was made of strong stuff and his mother made of even stronger. Or so his father always said.

"Crissy, you remember our son, Brock?" his father said, sitting again.

"I..." Her eyes narrowed slightly.

"I was the officer that found you," he said, not willing to verbalize that Daryl Collins, the man responsible for kidnapping and raping her, had been his partner. He hated to think of him by his first name and chose to push the relationship they'd had away. Which is why he thought of his ex-partner now as just Collins.

"Right." She glanced down at her daughter, and he instantly understood she didn't want to talk about what she'd gone through in front of the child.

Moving over, he sat across from them and motioned to Chester's case. "Are either of you allergic to cats?" he asked.

When Crissy shook her head and glanced towards the case, he thought for a moment he saw a smile.

"Chester is a big softy." He reached down and opened the door. His cat didn't disappoint. After strolling out of the case as if it was a grand hotel instead of a small box, he meowed loudly, walked over to greet both of his parents, then headed straight for Crissy's daughter.

Emma cheered happily and reached for the cat's fur.

"Easy," Crissy warned her daughter. "Gentle."

Emma had the rest of them laughing when she held up a single finger and pet Chester's fur softly with it.

"You can use your whole hand." Crissy smiled and Emma instantly complied. Chester, being no fool, knew exactly who was going to give him the most pets and quickly laid down next to Emma and Crissy. "Your parents have been talking about how you will be staying with us for the next month."

His eyebrows shot up as he looked over at his father. If his dad wanted him to be that close to her, then he must be convinced there was a credible threat.

"Yeah, I hope that's okay with you and Emma?" he asked.

When he mentioned her daughter's name, Crissy's eyebrows rose slightly. Instead of answering, she nodded slightly.

"Good, then it's all settled." His mother clapped and then stood back up. "Now, I've arranged for all of us to have dinner out on the deck. Brit is in the kitchen preparing some spaghetti, which I've been assured is Emma's favorite meal." His mother easily walked over and snatched the small child from Crissy's hands.

The fact that Crissy and Emma were comfortable with his mother doing so told him that it wasn't the first time.

Brit was another local he'd known all his life. His father had hired the woman as a part-time assistant when his mother had taken a fall off a small stepladder, trying to get something down from the top shelf.

"Shall we go see if dinner is ready?" his mother asked Emma cheerfully. The little girl squealed and held on as they made their way through the house.

His father leaned forward and lowered his tone. "I haven't filled Brock in on all the details yet, but I assure you, he's more than capable of guarding you and your daughter until we sort things out."

"Thank you," Crissy said as her eyes moved to her balled fists. "The calls are coming closer together."

"Calls?" Brock jerked slightly and then looked at his father. "You mentioned a call. Not calls."

His father glanced over at Crissy, who sighed slightly.

"The first one came almost a month ago. I... didn't want to bother Reggie or Kim. But when they started coming more often... along with..."—she closed her eyes— "more, I knew I needed to do something."

"More?" he asked, his anger for the situation growing.

Crissy's eyes met his. "Details. Ones that the police assured me they wouldn't release."

Brock glanced at his dad, who quickly nodded. "Which is why Joe agreed to send you to us," his father said easily. "Now, I'm sure the two of you will hash out everything later. Why don't we head out and enjoy the rest of the evening? The back deck is the best place in the Keys to watch the sunset." His father quickly disappeared, leaving the two of them alone.

Brock stood up quickly and noticed Crissy flinch ever so slightly. Damn. Taking a deep breath, he motioned with his chin.

"Ready?" he asked her softly, as one would a spooked animal.

He watched her chin rise ever so slightly before she nodded and stood up.

"More than ready," she said softly, and he got the hint that there was a double meaning in her words.

CHAPTER THREE

Crissy tried all through dinner not to stare at Brock. Oh, she knew exactly who he was. Knew of the man's struggles over the past two years.

Even though his struggles were far different than what she'd gone through, the man had suffered. He'd been betrayed too, just as Carl had betrayed her after everything she'd gone through.

So many in the media had pointed a finger at the partner of... she couldn't say or even think about her captor's name. How could any good cop, the media had asked, not know what was going on right under his nose?

There was even a time when Brock had been questioned about his involvement. Months later, when he was fully cleared, the media had started calling him a hero when they'd discovered it had been one of his bullets that had killed his partner and, more importantly, that he'd been the one to discover her. Suddenly, the media couldn't get enough of the sexy cop partner of the crazed serial killer.

Brock Miller's face had been on every tabloid along the eastern coast of Florida. They were even talks of making a made-for-television movie about his life. Then again, there had been talks about doing one of her, and that of both Emily and Jamie. Her story and Jamie's were the hottest topics since she was the one who lived, and Jamie was the one who had killed one of the now infamous Miami serial-killer brothers.

Thankfully, the talk of making movies had died down with time.

Brock looked even more handsome in person. She remembered him from that night when he'd rescued her. Remembered hearing his soft tone as he promised her that she was safe. Then she'd woken in the hospital almost a week later.

Watching Brock laugh and joke with his parents had her relaxing around him even more. He was not a serial killer. That she was extremely sure of deep down in her core.

She'd read every article about him since that night. She'd followed his career and his personal life as much as she could.

She didn't know if his parents had offered her the job out of their guilt and kindness or if Brock had anything to do with the deal.

Watching the family interact, something told her it was the latter. No matter the case, she understood the Millers to be kindhearted people who would have gladly hired her regardless of her past experiences working in a strip club.

Sitting on the massive deck that hung on the back of the large home and overlooked the clear emerald waters of the Gulf of Mexico, she felt as if she could finally relax for the first time in a month.

She knew that she should have contacted Reggie after that first call.

But she'd talked herself into believing she was just being a hysterical victim once more. In the first year, she'd jumped at every shadow. It had taken all her strength and willpower just to step foot outside, much less go to a grocery store. She'd sheltered Emma too much and hadn't allowed her daughter to meet other kids her own age.

Moving to the Keys had been a blessing to both of them. She loved hearing Emma giggle when Brock picked up his cat, which had been begging at his feet, and made it ask for a bite of Emma's spaghetti in a funny voice. Her daughter eagerly complied by giving the cat an entire meatball.

Chester quickly snatched the thing and gobbled it whole. When Emma tried to give the cat another one, Brock laughed and set the cat down. "I think one is enough for tonight."

Crissy knew that her daughter was done with the meal when her eyes started drooping and a big yawn almost toppled her over.

"I think it's time we headed home," she said when the conversation died down.

"Right." Brock nodded and then stood up and gathered everyone's empty plates.

"Thank you for coming out here," Kim said as she wiped Emma's face and hands.

"Thank you for having us and thank you for..." Crissy felt a lump in her throat. "Everything else."

Kim smiled. "We'll get Emma's car seat from my car and put it in Brock's Jeep. If it's okay, since he'll be staying there, he'll drive you back instead of us."

Crissy nodded. "Thanks."

Emma had fallen fast asleep the second Kim had placed her in the car seat in Brock's newer model Jeep. The two of them rode in silence for a while until she felt the urge to thank him grow too strong.

"Thank you," she blurted out as they turned onto her street.

"For?" he asked, not removing his eyes from the road.

"For..." She felt her stomach turn. "Everything."

"Don't thank me," he said after a moment of silence.

"Why not?" she asked, feeling slightly shunned somehow.

He pulled into the parking lot of the pool house and waited until he'd turned off the Jeep before answering. "Because I didn't do anything."

"Yes, you did," she said, turning slightly towards him. "You came all this way to stay here because..." She swallowed as she shook her head. "Your job, your home... uprooting your cat." She nodded to the animal carrier sitting next to her daughter.

Upon that Brock smiled and then laughed. "You're a surprise."

Her eyebrows shot up. "I am?" she asked with a slight frown.

"Yeah." He nodded and without any further explanation, opened his door. "I'll get Emma, if you'll get Chester?" He nodded to the cat's carrying case.

For the next few minutes, they shuffled Emma and his things past the main house and into the pool house.

When his parents had come up with the idea of having him come down there to watch out for her and Emma, they had wanted to cancel all of the bookings until further notice so he could stay in the bigger house. But there was no way she would have allowed them to lose so much money because of her.

Instead, she'd offered to have Brock stay in the pool

house with her and Emma while they hunted down the sick person responsible for the phone calls. After all, there was an entire guest room that she and Emma didn't use.

"Where's her room?" Brock asked, standing in the doorway to the guest room.

"Upstairs," she answered. She set Chester's case down inside the guest room.

"Not in here?" he asked, looking around.

"No, she likes it up there." She started to reach for her daughter.

"I've got her," Brock said easily, and he started towards the narrow set of stairs that led up to the loft.

She followed him and hid a smile when he had to duck at the top so he didn't bump his head on the ceiling.

Emma's bed was in the far corner and just watching the six-foot man make his way across the room entertained her. She was short enough that she didn't have to bend over to walk around the loft area.

She stood back as he gently laid her daughter in the bed and then sat and removed her shoes.

"You're good at this. Do you have any kids of your own?" she asked, already knowing the answer but needing him to say it. She walked over to the dresser and pulled out one of her daughter's nightgowns.

"No, my sister Amber has two girls." He stood back up and let her start removing Emma's outfit.

"Right." She nodded and felt like a fool. She'd met his sister and her family a few times. They'd come down from North Carolina and had spent time at the rental.

"This is a pretty cool play area," he said, looking around. "Not for anyone over six foot, but for a kid, not bad." He nodded. "We used this area for storage when we lived here."

She glanced over her shoulder. "You... lived here?"

"For a summer." He shrugged. "While Dad and I built the house." He nodded to the window and the bigger home across the pool area.

"The two of you built the house yourselves?" She tucked her daughter under the blankets. Emma instantly turned and started sucking her thumb.

Crissy gently tugged the thumb out of her mouth and smiled when Emma jerked it back into her mouth.

"Yeah, along with my sister's husband, Leo. Of course, Leo could only help out a few months when school was out. He's a principal of a grade school."

"Yes, I remember," she said with a smile as she stood next to him.

Brock motioned for her to head down the stairs first. It was strange, being so close to a man again. Her entire body was very conscious of his at all times.

She'd felt an almost instant pull of attraction to him when he'd walked into the room at his parents' place, something she hadn't felt in years. She had been prepared to never feel it again. She was far better off denying her body and her needs. She hadn't wanted to think about how she would react to any sexual scenario after...

She reached the bottom step and turned quickly to tell him good night, but she'd misjudged, and he bumped directly into her.

His hands went up to her shoulders to steady her as their bodies bumped together.

"Sorry," he said under his breath. Her eyes snapped to his. They were a dark caramel brown. So unlike Carl's or... anyone else's she'd known.

She found herself instantly sinking deeper into them.

"For?" she asked, not really thinking.

Sadness washed over his features so quickly.

"Everything," he answered, his voice cracking slightly. "Everything," he said again with a shake of his head. Then his hands were gone from her shoulders, and he stepped away quickly, causing her to sway slightly. "I'll…" He looked around. "I'll see you in the morning." He picked up his bag and disappeared into the guest bedroom, leaving her standing in the living room alone.

Since the month was up, the current guests were due to leave first thing in the morning. She knew that her evening wasn't quite over yet. There was a large closet of freshly laundered linens in the main house, as well as the supplies she needed to clean the place. She left it up to the guests how often they wanted her to clean. Most guests enjoyed having a maid of sorts during their month-long stay. Some even preferred she cleaned every single day. She didn't mind. It usually made the switch out easier, so she didn't have to do a huge sweep in one day.

She also handled the paperwork and accounting side of the business, which kept her busy sometimes until late at night. She tended to do most of that work after Emma went to bed. Partially because it was quiet, but mainly because it took her a few hours to settle down herself. She needed distractions from her thoughts, and crunching numbers distracted her easily enough.

She usually sat on the sofa and used the small laptop to do all the work, but tonight she gathered everything up and disappeared into her own bedroom.

She could hear Brock moving around in his room, heard him talking softly to the cat. She wanted to tell him that he could let Chester roam freely, but figured she'd wait until the morning to do so.

Once all the accounting was caught up, she peeled off

her clothes, donned a swimsuit, and stepped out into the warm night air for her nighttime swim.

The pool was just large enough that she could enjoy a few laps. She'd been on the swim team in high school and was really enjoying having a place to swim again.

"You look like you do that a lot," a deep voice said when she stopped at the edge of the pool for a sip of water. She gasped and turned to see Brock sitting in one of the lounge chairs near the edge of the pool. She didn't know how long he'd been there, but by the looks of how relaxed he was, it had been a while.

"Swim team in high school," she answered, trying to settle her heart down.

She hated that she could be spooked so easily. Hated that even now, after two years, the fear was so easily invoked.

Brock nodded. "I was on the team for a year before being kicked off," he said with a smile.

She crossed her arms and rested her elbows on the side of the pool. "For?" she asked, putting her chin on her arms.

"Let's call it flirting with the coach's daughter," he joked.

"Oh?" She smiled.

"Laura was my first love." He put his hand over his heart. "Until I started dating Sarah. Or was it Stephanie?" He shrugged.

"Something tells me you were incorrigible." She laughed.

"Believe it or not, Key West is a small town. Our graduating class had fifty people in it. It was my responsibility to spread the love," he joked as he stood up and walked towards the edge of the pool.

Her breath caught when he peeled off his shirt,

exposing a hard body with a perfect six-pack. He jumped effortlessly into the water.

When he surfaced, his dark hair was slicked back, giving her an unhindered view of his face. He really was one of the sexiest men she'd ever seen.

Carl had been pudgy from the moment she'd met him back in high school. It had taken her a few years to warm up to his looks. But looking back on their relationship, she believed that, more than anything, she'd fallen in love with the attention he'd given her.

He'd been her out from the almost daily beatings.

"Where'd you go to school?" Brock asked her as he treaded water beside her.

"North Miami," she answered, and when he nodded slightly, something told her that he'd already known that.

"Do you like it here?" he asked, watching her.

"Yes," she answered quickly. "Why did you decide to head to Miami?"

"I thought I wanted to be where the action was," he answered after a pause.

"Thought?" she asked. "Past tense?"

His eyes locked with hers. "Yeah, past tense."

# CHAPTER FOUR

Brock hadn't known what to do when Crissy had walked right past him earlier and jumped into the water. It was dark, and he'd been sitting in one of the lounge chairs after getting off the phone with his dad.

He'd stepped outside so as to not disturb Crissy, whom he'd thought had been fast asleep. After all, it was a quarter past eleven already.

But after his father had finished filling him in on the details of the calls she'd been receiving, he'd sat outside and had been on the verge of falling asleep under the stars when she'd stepped outside in a sleek once-piece swimsuit and effortlessly slid into the pool.

He'd watched as she'd glided through the pool with even strokes and thought about everything she'd been through. How could a person recover from such a thing?

How could she, even now, swim through the water and not break into a million pieces? She had to be one of the strongest humans he'd ever met.

He'd watched her smile at her daughter during dinner and wondered just how she did it.

For him, the weight of what Daryl and his half-brother Scott had done to all those women dragged him down. Sure, there were moments he lost track of what had happened, but then it would come crashing back and the darkness would almost consume him once more.

Even now, after countless sessions with a counselor, he still struggled to trust anyone else. Which is why he'd gone through more than a dozen partners at work in the past year.

"Where are you thinking about going now?" she asked, kicking off from the edge of the pool.

"Not sure yet," he answered. "My dad has apparently been trying to get me back here for some time."

"Oh?" she asked, and he watched her suck her bottom lip between her teeth.

"Rumors are that my dad's thinking about retiring," he continued. "My chief thinks he's vying for me to take the reins and run for the position."

"Is that something you want?"

"I haven't really thought about it," he admitted. "I suppose if there was reason enough for me to stick around." He shrugged. "What about you?" he asked suddenly, and her eyes went large.

"Me?" she said finally.

"Sure. Are you planning on sticking around the Keys indefinitely?"

"Oh, sure. Yeah." She swallowed. "We love it here. I don't think I've been anywhere else where I feel so at home."

He smiled. "If you can get past all the tourists and chickens," he joked.

She smiled. "I rather like the chickens. The tourists..."

She shrugged. "They help pay the bills." She motioned towards the larger house.

"Right." He nodded. "How's that work anyway?"

"What? The job?" she asked, and he quickly nodded. "Oh, well, I do everything that's needed for the place to run smoothly."

"Bookkeeping?" he asked, and she nodded. "Cleaning? Cooking?"

"Cleaning, yes. No to the cooking. Most of the guests eat out or enjoy grilling and cooking for themselves and their families."

"How does Emma like living here?" he asked, already guessing that the little girl probably loved it. The loft area had been transformed from the storage area it had been the last time he'd been in the space into a dream playroom that any little girl would wish for.

"She loves it. Her best friend Tilly lives next door, she has a wonderful space to grow and learn in, and a pool in her yard." Crissy smiled.

He couldn't help but smile along with her. They grew silent for a few moments.

"I know you're tired from the long drive today, but we should probably talk about...." She sighed. "How this is going to work."

"How is what going to work?"

"This." She waved between them. "What do I tell the customers arriving tomorrow?"

He shrugged. "Tell them whatever you want." He meant it. He didn't want to cause her any discomfort, but other people's opinions were currently at the bottom of his list of worries.

The topmost item was protecting Crissy and Emma and finding whoever was doing this to her.

"Well, since you'll be staying in the pool house..." She bit her bottom lip. "I could say that you're family?" She looked at him and he frowned. "Or not," she added quickly.

"Why do you have to say anything?" he asked.

"People ask."

"They ask about your personal life?" he asked. When she nodded, he added, "And you answer them?"

"Sometimes." She shrugged. "Most are just curious about the dynamics of..." She motioned to the pool house. "When they rent the house, it's clear that the property manager and family live in the pool house and have free rein of the pool and yard area. They're just curious most of the time."

"Okay, so why say anything at all. Tell them what you normally do. Let them assume whatever they want."

She dipped her chin under the water and then nodded. "Okay."

"Since we're on the subject... Want to fill me in on anything else you can remember about the calls?" he asked. Instantly, her eyes and her mood darkened.

Again, he waited while she thought for a moment.

"The voice is deep. Almost... as if he was trying to make it much deeper than it normally is," she said slowly.

"Okay." He nodded, making a mental note. "Did he speak with an accent? Southern or... anything you could discern?"

"No. Possibly a slight lisp around the S's. But... I'll have to listen for it next time."

"So, you believe the calls will continue?" he asked.

She nodded quickly. "Without a doubt." She pushed through the water towards the stairs and the shallower part of the pool. He followed her and they both sat on the shelf area. She hugged her knees to her chest as he leaned back against the wall.

"He's been pretty steady for the past few weeks," she finished.

"And you just told my father about the calls today?" he asked. "Why now?"

She glanced over at him. "Do you know how many calls like this I've received over the past two years? Sick men thinking what I went through was simply a joke or, worse, a lie told to cover up an affair I'd had. Some even believe there weren't any murders at all. They think it's some sort of conspiracy to make the police look bad because..." She dropped off and averted his eyes.

He clenched his back teeth together, remembering standing in the doorway, seeing his partner lying dead on the floor after he'd kidnapped Jamie Garner, the woman who had been kidnapped by Daryl's half-brother, Scott Alcott a year earlier. Jamie had luckily escaped and in the process had killed Scott.

He remembered the sick feeling when they'd discovered the first body on Alcott's property after finding Crissy alive in that shipping container. They'd discovered eleven more bodies buried around the grounds in the following weeks and months. Even now, the land around the massive property was still checked thoroughly after storms, just in case something new was unearthed. DNA from both men was found all over most of young woman that had been discovered.

Four of the bodies only had Collins's DNA, which meant that his partner had kidnapped, raped, and killed four women in the year after his half-brother had gone missing. Crissy had been his fifth victim.

"Well," he finally said.

"Most of the calls I can brush off... after a while. It

shocks me, always does at first." She looked up into the dark night sky. "But after a while, I convince myself that it's just someone trying to get a thrill. There are those that love pushing a victim around and"—she quickly glanced in his direction— "I refuse to be a victim again after that day."

"Good for you," he said with a nod. "What set this call apart from all those others?"

She turned her face away again and bit her bottom lip. "He knew things that the others didn't."

"Such as?" He hated to ask, but he had to know what he was working with. Was this sicko just another man trying to, as she said, push a victim around?

"He knew about my tattoos," she finally said. His eyes moved to the large floral tattoos on her shoulders. "Not these," she said, running her fingers over the area.

He glanced at her and frowned. "I don't see..." His words dropped off when she glanced at him with raised eyebrows, and suddenly he understood. Whatever other tattoos she had were private. "Okay, so it's someone you've been with before?"

She shook her head. "I've only been with one man." She made a strange little gasp and then shook her head as she closed her eyes. "Before..."

He understood again. She'd only slept with her ex-husband, Carl, before being kidnapped and raped by Collins. He instantly wanted to kill his partner again.

"Okay, so... maybe someone who was able to get their hands on a police report?" he suggested, and her face paled.

"They... have pictures of me?"

God! He was an idiot. "Hey..." He reached out to touch her shoulder, but she jerked away and stood up as she wrapped her arms around herself.

"Oh god! Have you seen..."? She shook her head as tears

started rushing down her cheeks. "Oh god!" She stumbled to get out of the pool.

He made a move to help her, but she jerked away.

"Don't!" she said, holding out her hands. "I... can't..." She shook her head. "Goodnight." She rushed to gather the towel she'd dropped by the deep side of the pool.

He watched her go and silently cursed himself. After a while, he decided to swim a few laps himself. He was too upset at his serious lack of judgment to fall asleep anyway.

The morning sunlight in his face woke him, and for a moment he forgot where he was. Then he heard a rooster crowing and everything from the day before flooded back to him.

God, he was an idiot. He kept his eyes closed to the sunlight and the world.

He needed to apologize to Crissy. To explain to her that most of the pictures in her file were just of bruised or broken body parts. There weren't any of... anything too intimate and private. Yes, he remembered seeing that tattoo of a bloody black crow holding a fragile white flower.

In truth, she looked so different than she had that last time he'd seen her that he almost fooled himself into believing she was a different person.

"Did you sleep here?" a soothing woman's voice asked, causing him to open his eyes.

He was on one of the cushioned lounge chairs by the side of the pool.

Crissy stood at the foot of the chair, a basket of laundry in her hands as she looked down at him.

"I did."

"Why?" she asked with a slight frown.

"I suppose because it was comfortable, and my clothes

were wet. Besides, I figured I'd disturbed you enough last night as it was."

Her frown increased. "You didn't upset me," she said with a slight shrug. "I suppose I should have known there would be photos for evidence."

"I promise you there wasn't anything... private."

Her chin went up slightly before she nodded her head. "Well, why don't you head inside and shower. I'm just going to go throw these in the wash before I make some breakfast."

"I can cook," he suggested as he got up out of the chair.

Her eyebrows arched. "If you want. Emma loves French toast and scrambled eggs."

He smiled at her. "I make the best French toast and scrambled eggs."

She narrowed her eyes. "We'll see." She turned around sharply and disappeared into the main house.

# CHAPTER FIVE

C rissy had a few quick things to take care of before she took Emma over to Beth's for the morning. Rushing around and double-checking the state of the rental was normally a pleasant task. But this morning, it seemed... mundane.

The real cleaning would happen after she dropped Emma off next door. For now, she checked for damage and made sure all of the furniture, decorations, bedding, and towels were still there. She'd learned her lesson after a large group of young adults had made off with several smaller items once she'd refunded them their deposit, and now she regularly checked these items.

When she walked back into the pool house via the back hallway door, Emma was just climbing onto one of the bar stools. Crissy noted that she was still wearing her pajamas. Brock was standing at the stove, flipping French toast in the pan. He had obviously done it a million times.

He'd changed into a new pair of board shorts and a different T-shirt and even appeared to have taken a shower, since his hair was still slicked back.

Neither of them had heard her come in yet, so she stood just inside the doorway and watched and listened. The easiest way to gauge a person was to see how they responded to a child's silly questions. And she knew her daughter was full of silly questions.

"Whatshadoing?" Emma asked, leaning on the stool to get a better look at Brock.

"Making French toast and scrambled eggs," he answered easily as he flipped the toast.

"Why?" Emma asked.

"Because your mama told me you like them," he answered easily.

Emma's eyes narrowed slightly. "Why?"

"Why did she tell me?" He glanced over his shoulder in Emma's direction and when she nodded, he shrugged. "Because I think she wants you to like me."

"Why?" she asked again.

He smiled and Crissy's heart skipped a beat. Damn, the man was sexy when he smiled. "Because I'm going to be staying here for a while," he answered her daughter.

"Why?" Emma asked again.

Here, she saw him pause. She could tell that he was stuck with trying to figure out what to tell the little girl.

"To help your mama out for a while," he finally answered after setting a plate of toast and eggs in front of Emma.

Good answer, Crissy thought.

"Doing what?" Emma asked, picking up her fork. "Mama usually cuts my toast," her daughter said with a slight pout, setting the fork back down.

"Okay." Brock easily picked up the fork and cut the toast into smaller pieces. "Better?" he asked, holding out the fork.

"Why does my mama need help?" Emma asked after taking the first bite.

Just then, Crissy decided it was time to step inside. She'd forgotten to set the laundry basket in the laundry room and instead set it down on the table.

"Because there are some things even your mama can't do on her own," she answered Emma easily as her eyes met Brock's.

"Why?" Emma asked between bites.

"Enough whys. Eat your breakfast so you can go play with Tilly." Crissy smiled. "She'll why you to death," she told him with a slight roll of her eyes.

"My nieces are the same way." Brock handed her a plate of toast and eggs. She spun the plate around as if inspecting the food. "Approve?" he asked.

She shrugged. "I saw Oliver do that at his restaurant once. I have no clue why, but yes, it looks delicious."

"Who's Oliver?" He gave her a sideways glance.

"Tilly's daddy," Emma chimed in.

"Right." He nodded and smiled.

"They live next door," Crissy supplied as she took her first bite of the food. "Not bad," she admitted, waving her fork.

"I like it, Mama," Emma said, nudging her with her elbow.

"It's good. Maybe we will have Brock cook breakfast for us all the time?" Crissy suggested to Emma.

"Yeah!" Emma cheered.

Brock laughed as he sat down next to Crissy with his own plate of food.

"So, what's the plan for the day?" he asked her.

"Well, Emma will head off to Tilly's after breakfast, until around eleven, so I can get the rental ready for the new guests, who will arrive around ten. Then its lunchtime, followed by a nap," Crissy said.

"I like naps," he broke into her thoughts.

Crissy giggled, and Emma frowned and said, "I don't."

"But we take them, just the same," Crissy added. "Then we have playtime followed by reading time, and then chores. Then we make dinner and have more story time. We usually sneak in a swim after dinner. If we can."

"Sounds like a busy day," he commented.

"What are you doing?" Emma asked him.

"Well, I'll help out where I can." He turned to Crissy. "What can I do to help?"

She looked at him, thinking for a moment. "I thought... don't you have... something you need to do?"

He shrugged. "Nope. I'm here. It's where I'm supposed to be."

"Okay," Crissy said slowly. "I suppose you can help with my Crazy List items." She motioned to the paper on the refrigerator.

"Crazy List?" He got up and took the list from the fridge.

"Yeah, it's my list of things that, if I'm crazy bored enough, I'll get around to doing." She smiled.

He read over the items and smiled. The list contained things like touch-up painting, sanding a rocking chair, changing a light bulb on the front porch, nailing down a loose board on the porch, and other odd jobs that she'd put off for a while.

"This is perfect." He set the list down and went back to finishing his meal. "I'll start these later today."

"Thank you," Crissy replied. She thought quickly then added, "Chester can roam the house. If he wants."

Brock smiled again. "He's already on that. He's exploring somewhere."

"So, what do you and Tilly do together?" he asked Emma.

"Watch cartoons and play," Emma answered with a shrug.

"What kinds of cartoons?" he asked her.

"Recorded ones. Mama doesn't like me watching television. Tilly's mama has to record them, but I like them all so very much," Emma finished with a heavy sigh, and Crissy felt her stomach roll at the possibility of having to explain why to Brock.

Instead, he quickly glanced over at her and gave her a weak smile, then started asking her daughter what her favorite cartoon was.

After breakfast, he convinced Crissy that he'd clean up while she dressed and walked Emma next door. This gave her some time to think as she cleaned the rental.

She heard him working outside, possibly on the rocking chair, but didn't stop to look and see what he was doing. After all, he and his father had built this entire house. Almost two hours later she stepped back outside, a bouquet of fresh flowers and a thank-you note the last group had left on the table in her hands.

She loved flowers. Loved that the family had thought to give her a little something extra. Sometimes she received cash tips. More often than not, she wasn't even acknowledged.

Brock was sitting in one of the chairs just outside the pool house. He had a laptop in his lap and a notepad on the coffee table in front of him.

"Do you have a moment?" he asked her, nodding to the chair next to him.

"Sure." She set the flowers on the table in front of them before sitting down next to him.

"Do any of these names ring a bell to you?" He handed her the notepad.

She felt her stomach drop as she looked over the long list. When not a single name jumped out at her, she handed it back to him with a slight shake of her head. "Should I know any of them?"

He frowned down at the notepad. "These are all the people who have accessed your case photos."

She stiffened and glanced down at the list in his hands. Pushing the panic attack back, she forced herself to breathe slowly. She held out her hands and he handed her the list once more. This time, she went over each name more slowly, forcing herself to really think about each name.

"No." She leaned back in the chair. "None of the names ring a bell." She set the list down on the table this time. "What does that mean?"

"Nothing," he assured her. "It was just the first step."

"What's the second one?" she asked, curious of how much more she could handle. How much more she could hide her emotions from him. After all, she didn't want to make him feel... well, beholden in any way.

"Tracing the calls that come in. My dad has already put a trace request into the court for the number here. With any luck, it's active already."

She shook her head slightly, not fully understanding. "Trace? Like they do in the movies?"

He laughed. "Yeah, only we won't need you to stay on the line to trace the call. We're just looking for the number he's calling from. Then we'll go from there. Most likely, it's a teenager just looking for thrills."

"But... the details that he knew," she reminded him. She

felt sick to her stomach, remembering the voice describe her own body to her in such detail.

"Cops have been known to leave case files lying around," he assured her with his calm tone.

She turned slightly towards him, frowning as she remembered how he must have felt after all those reports that said he should have known what his partner was doing right under his nose.

"Cops can be bad too," she said softly, trying to encourage him. She reached out and touched his hand softly. "Whatever happened to me and the others... it wasn't your fault."

He took a deep breath and turned his eyes away from hers, towards the calm waters of the pool.

The sound of her phone chiming caused them both to jump slightly.

"That'll be our new guests." She got up. He stood up suddenly as well.

"I'll greet them with you," he said, not leaving her a chance to deny him as he started walking towards the front gate.

"I can—" she started, but he stopped and turned towards her.

"From now on, I'm by your side anytime new guests arrive," he said in a low tone. "It's just part of my service," he added with a grin.

She smiled and nodded. "Fair enough." She motioned and they continued down the pathway on the side of the larger home towards the front gate.

"I'll be adding some more security cameras soon." He motioned to the side of the house. "I noticed that there are a few blind spots."

She nodded again. "I'll let the new guests know you'll

be doing some updates while they're here." She smiled towards the family standing on the other side of the large iron gates.

Instantly, she knew the young family had nothing to do with stalking or terrorizing her. First off, they were so busy arguing about where they'd parked the car that she doubted they even knew she existed.

Brock stood back and let her do her job and listened quietly to the well-planned speech that she made to new guests. She showed the couple around, then understood that they were just the first part of the group. Before they were done, Crissy's phone chimed signaling someone else had arrived at the gate.

"Continue here, I'll go greet the rest," he offered.

A few moments later, Brock showed the three other couples, with five more young kids, inside. These couples were happily chatting with one another as they lugged all their luggage inside while trying to keep their kids in line.

When everyone was inside, Crissy started her speech all over again and answered any questions the couples had about the area and the rental. Brock leaned against the door-frame and listened and watched her.

She really loved this part of her job—showing off the property, explaining the wonders and joys of the area. Seeing the excitement on the guests faces as they stepped out and saw the pool area.

Finally, while the family got settled, she and Brock stepped back outside and walked around the pool towards the pool house.

"It's obvious that you enjoy your job," he said easily. "I take it that this is a lot better than waiting tables?"

She stopped walking and turned to him. How many times had she feared someone would find out what she'd done for a living before they had moved there? So many times, she'd been looked down at by people for waiting tables in a strip club. Each and every person who knew her used it against her. Carl surely had, during the divorce, even when he'd been the one pushing her to take the job. He'd even pushed her to try out for a job stripping.

Brock knew where she'd worked. Knew all about... everything. Yet by the way he chose his words, she knew he wasn't looking down at her.

Before she could stop herself, tears filled her eyes, and she had to quickly look away in hopes of hiding those emotions.

# CHAPTER SIX

O h god! What had he said to cause her the tears? He scanned his memory. Tried to think of something he'd said that would have offended or hurt her.

Finding no fault, he reached out and touched her shoulder.

"I'm sorry," he said softly. "I... didn't mean..." he started, but she shook her head quickly and dashed her eyes dry.

"I... yes. I love my job." She stepped through the glass doors to the smaller place. He followed her and then stopped when she turned suddenly, almost toppling her over. His hands moved once more to her shoulders to steady her. She was so small. So... soft. Instantly, he wondered what she'd feel like pushed up against him. Then he shook that thought from his mind and dropped his hands and took a step back. "Why?" she asked suddenly, causing him to smile when it reminded him of Emma's questions a few hours earlier.

"Why what?" he asked.

"Why are you here? I mean, anyone could have helped me out. I get that your parents... I work for them and all, but why drop everything and come all the way down here?" She tilted her head as she looked up at him. "Please don't tell me it's guilt."

"No," he said softly. "Well, not all of it is guilt," he explained.

"Then what?" she asked, her eyes scanning his.

"Responsibility," he answered without thinking. This answer made her frown. A small crease formed at the upper corner of her lips.

"For me?"

"And Emma," he answered, still trapped within her haunting blue eyes. Without thinking about it, his hands had moved back up to her shoulders. "You probably don't remember, but I used to visit you in the hospital."

"You did?" she asked softly.

He nodded slightly. "I understand how your ex treated you and Emma after the divorce. Knew the horrors of what you'd gone through. Yes, guilt may have been the initial driving factor, but after a while... I just wanted..." He shook his head quickly. "No, I needed to know that you and Emma were okay."

He watched her swallow slowly, then to his surprise, her eyes moved down to his lips.

That move seemed to shake him out of his trance. Again, he dropped his light hold on her and this time took a giant step back.

He watched her face turn a slight pink just before she turned away from him.

"I... should get to work." She disappeared into the back hallway.

He stood there like a stupid statue made of marble as he listened to her tossing items into the washing machine.

Then, disgusted with himself for the gut reaction to kiss her, he turned and left.

After a trip to the hardware store and to the local police station to have a chat with his father, he returned to the house shortly before dinner.

He had hoped to have the new cameras installed, but he didn't want to disturb the guests while they enjoyed an evening by the pool. He figured he'd have plenty of time to put them up tomorrow.

Instead, he found Crissy and Emma enjoying some mac and cheese while they sat around the small kitchen table.

Upon seeing him, Emma smiled and grew excited.

"Brock, Brock, I made you something." She rushed to get off the chair.

Crissy glanced over at him while her daughter rushed over and grabbed a drawing off the refrigerator and handed it to him.

He squatted down and took the paper from Emma and noticed how excited the little girl was to see him.

"You made this for me?" he asked, looking at all the bright colors on the paper. To his eye, he couldn't see any patterns to the madness.

"Uh-huh." Emma nodded. "It's a picture of you helping Mama out." She smiled up at him and he grinned.

"Of course, it is." He held up the paper and, suddenly, he could see it clearly. The blue line was him, the red one Crissy. "Are we..." He squinted and guessed, "Doing laundry?"

"Yes!" She clapped cheerfully and then rushed back to her chair. "We're having Macheese," she said as she climbed back onto the chair with Crissy's help.

"Yeah, smells good," he joked.

"There's chicken and peas in it. I don't like the peas."

Emma frowned. "But I gotta have my veg." She rolled her eyes and made him laugh.

"Sorry, mac and cheese is Emma's favorite. If you want…" Crissy started to get up, but he stopped her by holding a hand up.

"I'm good with whatever. I can get a bowl myself." He assured her. "I don't want you feeling like you have to serve me." He waited until she nodded in agreement before walking over and getting some dinner for himself.

"I've never had mac and cheese with chicken in it before," he told Emma.

While they ate, Emma told him all about all the wonderful food she loved. Then when Crissy brought out a small cup of pudding, she explained all the desserts she loved as well.

"Okay, I think Brock is done hearing about all your favorite foods." Crissy laughed as she moved over to pick up her daughter. "I think it's bath time and then story time."

"No." Emma frowned, sticking out her bottom lip.

"Yes," Crissy countered. "Unless you want the tickle monster to get you." She tickled her daughter, who erupted into a fit of giggles as they disappeared down the hallway.

While he listened to the happy sounds coming from the bathroom, he pulled out his laptop and scoured through the list of people who had seen Crissy's file once more. He'd taken the time to type them into a datasheet and had added more information thanks to the meeting with his father. He now knew which people still had active logins into the system and which ones didn't.

More than a dozen people on the list were either retired or no longer with the force. Those were all highlighted in red as potentials. Three names were blacked out due to deaths. The rest of the names were highlighted in green.

He figured he'd go through and mark those that were local, just for ease.

He wanted to know just how close any of them were to Crissy and Emma.

The fact was, he hadn't even thought to put Crissy's ex-husband's name on the list until his father mentioned earlier that Carl Talbot had been arrested three times in the last year.

After Crissy had divorced the guy, Brock had lost all interest in looking out for the man. Until now.

Now Carl was the first name on his list. He hadn't realized that Crissy's father, Simon Jones, was still alive until his father mentioned him as well. Hell, he was doing a very bad job at figuring out who could be making these calls if her ex and her father hadn't even been on his initial radar.

A quick search on the man brought up no current address. Which is why he'd assumed the man was deceased.

"The man lives off the grid. You know the type. Refuses to let the government tell him what he can and can't do on *his* land. The guy's been squatting on the same property for years now. Every now and then, someone will go out and have a talk with him, but they always come back unable to find the guy." His father had read from the man's file. A file Brock now had a copy of.

When Crissy came back down after tucking Emma into bed, she joined him outside on the patio. The families had disappeared with the explanation that they were heading to dinner at a local restaurant.

"I bet you enjoy this time of night," he said to her.

She glanced over at him and frowned. "Not normally." She shook her head and gave a nervous little giggle. "The quiet and I don't get along well. I've even taken up painting and needlepoint to fill the time."

He felt like kicking himself. He'd gone through all the training about how to deal with victims of crime. How, even when the horrors were over, most lived the hell over and over again. It was a huge reason a lot sought the comfort of drugs, alcohol, or... final darkness.

"I'm sorry," he said again.

She turned a little more towards him. "You keep apologizing."

"I do?" He shrugged when he realized she was right. "Yeah, I guess I do. Sorry."

She smiled and then asked. "What about you? What do you do on your off time?"

"I run," he answered quickly. "Hit the gym." He shrugged. "Mostly, I don't have free time." He wanted to add that that had become the case in the past few years, since he'd found out that his partner had been raping and killing. But he held that part back. "Still, this is a far better view than my apartment next to an Indian food place."

"You live next to an Indian food place?" she asked, her eyes narrowing. "How often do you eat there?"

"I used to eat there twice a week. Now, since I smell it on my clothes and in my sweat, not so much," he joked.

"We used to live next to a pizzeria. I swear everything tasted like greasy cheese. I couldn't eat pizza for a whole year after we moved out."

"We? You and your ex?" he asked, hoping to transition the conversation to her father.

Her smile slipped. "No," she answered softly. "Me and my father."

"Is he still alive?" he asked, already knowing the answer.

She turned slightly and tilted her head. "Something tells me you already know the answer to that."

He sighed heavily and nodded. "I guess I'm not as subtle as I used to be."

She gave him a half smile. "You probably want to know about him?" He nodded and she continued. "I noticed his name and Carl's weren't on your list." She motioned to his computer screen.

"They are now," he assured her.

"Good." She nodded and turned her eyes to the palm trees and flowers in front of them. "As much as I'd like to defend them, I just don't have it in me any longer to stand up for men who..."

"Abused you?" he interrupted.

She jerked her head towards him. "In one way or another, yes," she said softly. "I can admit that now. Thanks to counseling."

"Good. Let's start with your dad."

"I need some wine if I'm going to open up." She stood up. "Do you want something to drink? I have some beer."

"Beer would be good." He nodded and watched her go back inside. He couldn't explain why he was so nervous about hearing her story. Maybe because he'd surmised that what she'd gone through on Collins's property hadn't been the worst of it. Maybe because he feared that, even though she appeared strong, she'd end up breaking, and he wouldn't be able to piece her back together again.

He knew that counselors were trained to talk victims like her through her past. To make them feel at ease. He wasn't a counselor. He was a cop. He was a man. He was... interested in her.

That last part jolted him. Twisted at his gut. He supposed that it was because over the past two years, a day hadn't gone by when he hadn't thought of her. Of finding her in that container. Of what she'd gone through. Of how she struggled to recover.

It was those thoughts that helped him get through all the troubles with the press. All the negativity he'd suffered due to his closeness to Daryl.

The one thing that had helped him through it all was that, no matter how bad he had it, he'd remind himself that Crissy had it worse. Just then Chester jumped up on the chair next to him, and he absently rubbed the cat's soft fur. Even his cat felt more at home here, he thought.

Since returning, he'd been wondering why he'd left. He loved it here. Loved the smell, the quiet, the ease of everything.

When Crissy stepped back out onto the patio holding a glass of wine and a beer, he felt his heart jump in his chest. She'd changed into a swimsuit and had one of those white flowing coverups on, the kind that was completely see-through. It showcased her sexy body and the little red swimsuit she had pulled on.

Instantly, he knew that if he was going to get through the evening without making a move on her, he was going to have to focus strictly on business. Using all of his training, he pushed his desires, his wants, aside.

Thinking that he could easily focus on her past, on the pain she'd been through, he held himself extremely still and did everything he could to avoid looking at her in that sexy outfit. Damn. She had a sweet little body he wished more than anything he could explore and enjoy.

# CHAPTER SEVEN

What did a woman have to do to get kissed? She'd gone out on a limb and had changed into the sexiest thing she had, a hot red two-piece swimsuit someone had left at the rental a few months back.

She'd hoped to detour his questions by giving him a beer and dressing in practically nothing. But instead, he took the beer and started rattling off questions about her father.

Did she know where he was? When was the last time she'd talked to him? When was the last time she'd seen him?

Brock hardly even looked in her direction. Instead, his eyes were glued to the can of beer, as if it was the most interesting thing within sight.

One thing that Dr. Rizzo had wanted her to try in her journey to recovery was to allow herself to enjoy the physical contact of others. Well, until now, she hadn't wanted any physical contact with anyone.

Before the kidnapping, she'd loved sex. Loved every part of making love with someone she'd been in love with. Carl hadn't been a terrible lover, just a selfish one at times.

Still, she'd enjoyed being with him enough that it had stung when he'd rejected her and pretty much ignored her after she'd recovered. Oh, not in the physical sense. Instead, he'd been annoyed that she hadn't wanted to jump right back in the sack with him.

It had taken her a while to fall out of love with Carl and she was sure that it reflected on her desires for him. Not to mention her sex drive. She was convinced that she'd lost that back in that shipping container.

Now, as she watched Brock take a swig of his beer, she imagined what it would be like to run her fingertips down his neck, over that sexy Adam's apple of his. How it would be to feel the scruff of his short beard on her chin, her lips, while she trailed kisses over his face.

What would it be like to have his hands on her?

She may not be ready to move onto the final act, but that didn't mean she couldn't enjoy playing a little. Just as long as she was in control, she told herself as she continued to daydream.

"And you are no longer paying attention to me," Brock broke into her thoughts.

Setting her wine glass down, she sighed. "Sorry, it's been a long day. How about we take a dip before the family gets back from dinner?" She stood up. She wanted to see his face as she peeled off the coverup but lost her nerve. Instead, she walked to the edge of the pool, removed the barrier quickly, and dove in the water.

When she surfaced, he was standing at the edge of the water, pulling off his T-shirt. Her eyes slowly ran over his arms, his chest, down lower to the sexy trail of dark hair that led her eyes below his bellybutton.

Then he jumped in the water next to her. The instant the cool water splashed over her, it shook her out of the trance of watching him. Her heart was beating so hard that she was sure that if she looked closely enough, she would see waves in the water coming from her body.

She swam closer to him, letting their bodies bump slightly.

"What are you doing?" he asked, his eyes slipping down to her lips.

"What do you mean?" she asked, biting her bottom lip.

His eyes narrowed as she moved closer to him. "You know what I mean," he said in a low voice as her body brushed up against his again.

She sucked in a breath and reached out and gently laid a hand on his chest under the water.

"Crissy," he warned, but she was moving even closer. Now their legs were tangled, and his hands wrapped around her waist as she continued to run her hand over his arms, his chest, lower.

She watched his eyes close. Heard a low moan. Felt it vibrating in his chest.

"I... haven't done this or wanted to..." She glanced down at his lips quickly. "Since... before." Her eyes moved slowly back up to his, which were watching her and filled with desire.

She felt him stiffen slightly at her admission and start to pull away from her, but she easily held him still in the waist-deep water.

"No, don't," she warned him. "This is good." She smiled. "Call it therapy. Call it..." She bit her bottom lip, then whispered, "An experiment." She finished right before she dipped her head and gently brushed her lips across his.

To his credit, he allowed her to slowly explore his mouth. She kept her hands firmly on his shoulders, but in the back of her mind, she dreamed of running them over his bare chest.

She felt his fingers tighten slightly on her hips as he pulled her closer. Skin slid against skin as she took the kiss deeper, enjoying the way he tasted and felt.

Then he was pulling away from her, and the removal of the warmth his body had provided against hers made her entire body shiver.

"I think the guests are back," he said in a low tone from a few feet away from her in the pool.

Then she heard it, the laughter of people. The banging of doors inside the house. Any minute now, she knew that they'd be stepping outside to enjoy the pool themselves.

"Right," she said with a smile. "We should..." She nodded to the pool house and then without waiting for a reply, climbed out of the pool. After pulling on the coverup, she didn't wait to see if he would follow her. She just grabbed her wine glass and retreated inside.

The moment the patio doors were shut behind Brock, he turned to her. "I... maybe we can finish our chat tomorrow?" he suggested.

"I didn't mean to scare you," she joked suddenly. She hated thinking that she'd spooked him, or worse, that he regretted the kiss.

"You didn't," he assured her. "It's just... I'm not sure what to expect." He ran his hands through his wet hair. "It would be easier if I knew what you can handle and what you can't."

She felt her heart skip and her knees turn slightly to jelly. "The fact that you care to ask assures me that I wouldn't have to fear that things would be awkward. Nor would I have to worry that you'd be angry if I needed you to stop."

His eyes went wide. "No, I wouldn't be angry. What kind of man would if they knew..."? He set down his empty beer can and the T-shirt that he'd been holding and walked over to lay his hands gently on her shoulders. "No, it won't be awkward between us." Then he smiled and she felt her knees weaken. "Actually, some men find it very exciting when a woman tells him what to do and what she wants."

She tilted her head. "Are you one of those men?"

His laughter had her smiling. "I can be. At times." He leaned closer. "Tell me you want me to kiss you," he said as his mouth hovered inches from hers.

"Brock," she said, locking her eyes with his, "kiss me." Then she held her breath as he covered her mouth gently with his.

When he stepped back and dropped his hands from her, she realized that at no point during their encounter that evening had she flashed back to her past. Either with Carl or... the darkness.

"You're good for me," she said softly, causing him to smile.

"Good." He nodded. "Now, I know you must be tired, since you started before five and it's..." He glanced over at the clock on the wall and winced. "It's past ten, so I'll let you get some sleep. Tomorrow, however, I'll need you to answer the questions about your father."

She felt her stomach sink but nodded in agreement.

"Good night, Brock," she said. She moved around to let Chester inside, then locked the doors and disappeared into her room.

When she crawled into bed, she pulled out her e-reader. Normally, it took her at least an hour to fall asleep, but tonight, before she reached the bottom of the first page, she was out.

It must have been her subconscious playing over the events of the evening when the dream—no, the memory—started. She watched it replay in her head like a movie.

Sure, she knew what to do. Dr. Rizzo had walked her through the steps of quashing nightmares. First, she had to realize that it was only a dream. Next, she had to tell herself that she was safe at home in her bed and that Daryl Collins was dead and could no longer terrorize her. Last, she had to take control of the dream and change the narrative.

But tonight, no matter what she did, she couldn't shake free.

She was back in the shipping container Collins had used for his and his brother's sick games, as he'd called what he had done to her.

Since Collins had been a police officer, he'd used his badge to pull unsuspecting women like her over. She hadn't remembered that part at first, but after a month of recovery, she'd flashed back to being pulled over on her way home and then being knocked unconscious when she'd rolled down her window to talk to the officer. She'd been so worried about paying for a ticket, she hadn't once thought to be afraid of the man.

Alcott, Collins's half-brother, had used a different tactic before he'd been killed. He drugged women in night clubs, like he'd done with Jamie the night she'd fought back and won.

Collins had taken her to a large property that Alcott had inherited just northwest of Miami. There were two large shipping containers on the land. One was full of junk of all sorts, the other was full of junk at the front, but the back was a cleared space where she had been kept. Back behind the facade of junk, there was a king-sized mattress where she'd been raped and beaten over and over for the week that she'd been held there.

She watched as if floating above the scene as Collins pulled her over. She was digging in her purse, pushing aside all her tips from that night waiting tables at the strip club, biting her lip, and praying that she could talk the officer into only giving her a warning.

When she woke up, she was in pain. Her head was spinning, and he was choking her as he used her body.

She'd fought. At first. But that only seemed to excite her captor. When she'd laid there, unmoving and uncaring, he'd threatened her life, cut her, broken her bones, anything to get a cry from her. So she'd gone back to fighting. But the damage had been done. She'd sensed that he'd grown bored of her.

She could remember him promising to end her suffering the next time he came to her. Which is why, when she heard the container door open, she'd welcomed the end. Only... instead of the blond-haired man with blue eyes that were full of evil, a uniformed officer with dark hair and kind sad eyes held out his hands and promised her with a gentle voice that she was safe.

Suddenly, her nightmare turned, and she was floating in the pool outside. All the pain was gone, along with the fear.

She watched Brock slowly remove his shirt before he jumped into the water. Then his dark eyes were glued to hers as his lips hovered over hers. Her entire body ached for him. She dreamed of enjoying herself once more. When he was inches from kissing her, the dream was interrupted by a loud shrill of the phone next to her bed.

Jerking awake, she answered the call with her standard greeting.

"Thinking of me, aren't you, bitch?" The deep voice had

her body tensing. "Yeah, I bet you dream of what we did to you. I bet you like to remember the time I was inside you. The time we were both inside you. We'd blindfolded you and when you didn't scream, we burned you." The breath was knocked from her lungs as a new memory played in her head. Yes. Just like he described it. That had happened. She'd pushed it to the back of her mind. Had believed that it was just one more sick game Collins had played. Only... now, she wasn't sure. "You were my first fuck. My first share. The first time I got my dick in a wet hole. You were supposed to be my first kill too, but that ship has sailed. God! I was looking forward to fucking you while choking you. Watching the life slowly drain from those blue eyes of yours." He laughed, then growled. "You won't have to wait much longer. I'm coming for you. Soon." The laughter caused her entire body to ice over.

Just then, her bedroom door swung open, and she would have screamed if Brock hadn't rushed in and jerked the phone from her hands and hung it up. Then he pulled her into his arms and held her while she wept.

# CHAPTER EIGHT

Brock held onto Crissy until he felt her drift off. He didn't know if she'd passed out from pure exhaustion or just fallen asleep. Either way, there was no way he was going to let her go. Not until she woke up and knew that she was safe again.

He'd heard every word of the call. Every single damned word. Why hadn't she just hung up on the guy?

Was it all true? Had there been a third person? Someone working with Collins and Alcott? Had they tag teamed raping her? Burning her?

There hadn't been any evidence of that that they'd known of. Then again, there was more DNA from the crime scene than had been accounted for. The working theory was that it was from more victims.

When his phone chimed, he shifted slightly and glanced down at the screen.

The text message was from his father.

"Got a number and location. Local PD en route. I'll keep you posted."

He shot off a text, "Thanks."

"Who is it?" Crissy asked in a whisper.

"My dad." He shifted until he could look down at her. "They've got a number and location. We'll know more in the morning." She nodded slightly. "Can you sleep?" he asked. When she shook her head, he sighed. "Yeah, me either."

"How about I make some cinnamon rolls?" she asked suddenly.

He looked back down at her. "Now?"

She glanced around his chest and shrugged after looking at the clock by her bed. "It's morning."

He looked at the clock and laughed. "Just."

"You're hungry, right?"

He thought about it and then nodded. "Sure, who would turn down cinnamon rolls?"

"Baking helps take my mind off..." She started but then stopped. "Things."

His arms tightened around her for a second before letting her go. She climbed out of bed wearing a pair of cotton shorts and a T-shirt, but still pulled on a thick robe and hugged it to her body, as if she were cold. He wanted to remind her that it was easily eighty degrees in the house but kept his mouth quiet as he followed her into the kitchen.

"Can I help?" he asked.

"No, sit." She motioned to the bar top. "Talk to me about..." She stopped herself as she pulled items from the pantry. "What happened to you and that girl?"

"What girl?" he asked with a slight frown.

"The one you were dating when... The media was always in your face about..." She finished after a slight shake of her head.

"Reagan." He sighed. "She didn't stick around once people started pointing fingers at me."

"That's too bad." She started putting ingredients into a large mixer. "Her loss. Have you dated since?"

"No," he answered. "I had thought that Reagan was the one." He glanced down at his hands and remembered putting a down payment on a ring he was sure she would like.

"Where you going to ask her to marry you?" Crissy asked. When he nodded, she shook her head. "Like I said, her loss."

"I know what the media says happened between you and Carl is nothing like what the court papers say," he said.

She stopped working and glanced over at him. "The courts had it right. The media are clueless." She shook her head.

"Yeah, I thought so. The conspiracy theorists out there worked overtime just to make up some bullshit about you."

She was quiet for a moment, then he was surprised to hear the sound of her chuckling. "One newspaper actually reported that I was pregnant with my alien lover's baby."

He smiled. "Yeah, I saw that one."

She smiled over at him. "It made me laugh and suddenly I realized that I shouldn't take any of the articles about me seriously," she said, and he nodded in agreement. "So why haven't you dated since?"

He shrugged. "I guess I haven't found anyone willing to put up with me," he answered, wanting to change the topic. "You mentioned you paint?"

"Yeah. I don't get much time to, but occasionally Emma will go to bed early."

"I'd like to see something you've done," he said as she turned on the mixer.

"Sure, it's there in my art cabinet." She motioned to a

large cabinet that sat off to the side of the living space. He walked over and opened the doors.

Inside was a magically large amount of art supplies. Everything from easels and paint to colored papers, yarn, and small containers of sparkles. All of it was color coordinated perfectly.

"Wow," he said, standing back and admiring the rainbow of colorful things.

She answered from behind him, "I saw something like that online and put this together for Emma and myself. We have so much fun with craft time. She loves to draw and wants to learn how to needlepoint, but she's not ready for that yet."

"They sell little kits for kids. You know, with big needles and easier patterns," he suggested. "My sister got some for her kids last Christmas," he said over his shoulder as he pulled out a small painting.

It was no bigger than his hand, but the image was so detailed. It was of some brightly colored homes he knew sat down the street from there. She'd even added a rooster standing in front of the white picket fence.

The next painting was a close-up of a pelican, followed by small colorful beach huts on the beach with surf boards sitting beside them. The next was of a tabby cat lying in the sun.

Each painting was no bigger than his hand yet full of details.

"These are amazing." He glanced over at her. "Do you sell them?"

She stopped rolling the dough and looked up at him before laughing. "No."

"Why not?" he asked. "I know for a fact that paintings like this will easily sell around here. Tourists eat things like this up. They're small enough to get home and remind them of their trip here."

She tilted her head. "I guess I never thought of it like that. I could only afford the small canvasses." She shrugged. "So I painted small."

He pulled out a few more of her paintings. Each one was more impressive than the last.

"You're quiet over there," she said, getting his attention.

"Just in awe." He set the paintings down and moved back over to sit at the bar and watch her as she put the cinnamon rolls into the oven. "If you bake half as good as you paint, the cinnamon rolls are going to be epic."

She smiled. "What hidden talents do you have?" she asked him, moving over to make a cup of hot tea. "Coffee?"

He shook his head at the offer and thought about her question for a moment. "I used to skateboard and surf."

"Skateboard?" She nodded. "Long board or short?"

"Both. I had a motorcycle in high school. It was cheaper than a car."

"When you live in paradise, you don't need a car," she said with a smile. "I don't have one."

"Yeah, I've been meaning to ask about that. How do you and Emma get around?"

"Key West has these wonderful things called side-walks and for farther trips, busses," she joked, and he smiled.

"Groceries?" he asked.

"We have a wagon. The store is only a few blocks away and we enjoy the walk." Crissy shrugged and then sipped her tea. "Not a coffee drinker?"

"I am, but I've been trying to cut back."

"Health issues?"

"No, just... being proactive. My dad has high blood

pressure. Which is why everyone has been bugging him to retire."

"It must come with the job," she said. "It can't be easy being police chief of a whole island."

He laughed. "It's a heck of a lot easier than Miami."

"Everything here is easier than Miami," she said with a slight sigh.

He hated to do it, but since they had the time without interruptions, he asked. "What about your dad?"

He expected her to look annoyed, but she just shifted and leaned on the counter a little more. "He moved to a property in Copeland shortly after Carl and I got married. I lost track of him for a while." She paused for a moment. "Until after I was in the news." Her eyes locked with his. "Then he got in touch with me at the hospital and started asking if I was going to get some sort of settlement. He claimed that if I did, he was due some of it after putting up with my shit for years."

He felt his anger wake. "Seriously?"

She sighed and took another sip of her tea. "I should have expected it. When I married Carl, my dad asked him for some compensation. You know, since my new husband would be stealing his cook and maid, he expected to be paid for the loss."

Brock thought about his own father and the stark contrast between the two men. The gentle, kindhearted man who had raised him had never asked for anything from his child, but Crissy's father had treated her like property. Something to be used and exploited.

"Have you heard from him since moving here?" he asked.

"Only once."

"Does he know where you are?"

She nodded. "There was this article..."

"Right," he groaned as he remembered the report in the popular paper. There was even a very grainy photo of Crissy walking on the sidewalk with Emma. Thankfully, the paper had blurred out the little girl's face. But everything else had been there, including the name and address of the rental and, most importantly, the connection to the owners. "What did he want then?" he asked.

"What he always wants. Money. Payback." She shrugged, then stood up and walked over to glance in the oven.

"Is there a chance that this is him?" he asked, hating to bother her further. Especially after he'd listened to that last call.

"No." She shook her head and leaned on the counter as she crossed her arms over her chest. "This was..." Her eyes locked with his. "Someone else. My father is motivated by money. Whoever is calling has alternative goals."

"Was what he said true?" he asked.

She took a moment before answering. She bit her bottom lip and appeared to be taking several deep breaths.

"Yes," she finally said.

"It wasn't in the reports."

"No." She shook her head as a single tear slipped down her cheek.

He was up and across the small kitchen. He wanted to reach for her, but she was holding herself so tense he was afraid she'd snap in two if he touched her.

"I'm sorry," he said softly.

"No," she quickly replied as she dashed the tears away. "Don't be. My psychologist assures me that talking about it helps."

"Does it?"

Her eyes locked with his. "You're the only person I've tried it on so far," she said with a slight smile.

He smiled. "I want to hold you."

She nodded. "I'd like that too." She walked into his arms.

"We'll finish this discussion later. After we're awake and have some food in us." He felt her shake her head.

"No, it does help. Talking about it." She pulled back slightly. "Besides, it's fresh in my mind, and I don't want to forget a thing."

"You don't have to. The call was recorded."

"It was?" She frowned.

"Yes, for now, all the calls are being monitored and recorded. Are you sure you want to talk about it now?"

She dropped her hands and, after glancing at the oven, she nodded. "We have fifteen minutes until those are done. It helps to set a time limit. Like my counseling sessions," she added with a weak smile.

"Okay." He nodded towards the sofa.

She smiled. "In here is fine." She walked over and sat back down on a barstool. He followed her.

After she took a sip of her tea, she started.

"I hadn't remembered. What he'd talked about. Not until he mentioned it. That's why it wasn't on any reports. There's a lot I'd blacked out."

"I've been told that it happens in cases like this," he added, and she nodded quickly.

"Yes, Dr. Rizzo has warned me that over my lifetime I'll remember more atrocities from that time." She sighed.

"I'm sorry," he said softly.

She nodded slightly and continued. "She also warned me about false memories. This isn't one of them."

"False memories?" He frowned.

"Brought on by triggers. Movies and images of violence can bring on false memories. Dr. Rizzo has explained how to spot them." Crissy shut her eyes and took several deep breaths. "I'd lost track of the hours. I didn't know if it was day or night since it was always dark in the container. I didn't even know I was in a shipping container. I remember waking up when I heard the door open. It always caused a loud squeaking noise when it was opened and shut. That sound still haunts me." Her eyes opened and focused on a spot across the room. "He came in."

"Collins?" he asked.

"Yes." She closed her eyes again and took another deep breath. "He joked about having some new kind of fun. He unchained me from the wall."

He remembered the huge eyebolt she'd been chained to. Her wrists had been cuffed with four sets of police handcuffs, which had been looped through a thick chain. So thick, he doubted that Crissy had been able to even lift her hands because of the weight. Her wrists were cut deep from trying to free herself, clear down to the bone in places. He glanced down at her wrists now and could see the thin white scars.

"He carried me over to the mattress and chained me to them like he always did, my hands high above my head, cutting off the circulation. But then he stood over me and just looked down at me. When he pulled out a black pillowcase, I thought that this was it." Her eyes moved to his face. "Finally, I'd be free of him."

He swallowed the bile that threatened to surface. He wanted to be there, standing in his partner's home, gun aimed at his chest, firing bullets into his body all over again. How had he allowed the evil creature to fool him? He should have seen it there in the man's eyes as he joked about finding some new hottie to bang.

He'd always hated how Collins had talked about women, but a lot of men joked like that in the station. Not him. His mother's face and kindness always reminded him that no one should ever disrespect women.

"What happened?" he asked, knowing that she needed to continue.

"He put the hood over my head. Then...the same thing that he always did when he came to me." She frowned. "Or so I thought. This time, there were two of them. I'd thought it was some sort of... toy or tool at first." She closed her eyes and a tear slipped down her cheek. He watched her dash it away as if it was nothing more than an annoyance. "They joked about how to position me so that they could both work on me." Her eyes met his. "I was twisted and shoved, then eventually bent up almost into a headstand. I stopped fighting after they'd stretched and slapped at every part of my body..." She pulled the neck of her shirt aside and showed him a white puffy scar. "That was when I got this." Her eyes locked with his for the first time since she'd started the story. "They burned me until I screamed as they laughed."

## CHAPTER NINE

Just trying to go through her normal routine and keep her thoughts away from the darkness was extremely hard that day.

The terror kept sneaking in. She was out watering the plants, a task she loved to do each day, but her mind kept playing over the phone call. Over the memories. Over telling Brock what had been done to her.

She no longer felt ashamed or embarrassed, thanks to her time with Dr. Rizzo.

She was taking a potted plant to the front porch through the side gate when she heard the sound of the rusty hinge on the gate. The resemblance to the door on the shipping container startled her enough that her hands shook. She had to sit on the front porch swing for a full two minutes before she finally got her breathing under control.

Around lunchtime, Brock made her and Emma hamburgers on the porch grill while she read Emma her favorite book. This was the only time during the day where she wasn't worrying or remembering.

When Emma was down for a nap, Brock asked to speak to her outside.

"Sit," he said, motioning to the cushioned chairs that sat in the shade of the smaller porch on the back side of the pool house. The porch was surrounded by a jungle of green that separated it from the main pool area and gave it the privacy that she required. She sat down and held her breath, waiting.

"I just got off the phone with my father," he said, touching her arm. "The call last night came from an abandoned warehouse just outside of Miami."

She could see it in his eyes before he said it. Knew that something bad had happened. Knew that everyone understood that these weren't just prank calls any longer.

"And?" she asked, wrapping her arms around herself but feeling the chill seep in.

"They discovered a body." He took her hand in his. "We're trying to ID her."

"Her?" she asked and closed her eyes.

"Yes, from the looks of it, the police think it's a seventeen-year-old girl that went missing two days ago while walking home from school."

"Was she... Was it like what happened to me?"

He nodded. "It appears so. There were burn marks. Like..." He nodded to her shoulder, and she felt her stomach lurch. Taking several deep breaths, she willed her body back under control.

She remembered his words last night. "He promised me I'd be his first kill. He said that ship had sailed..." She looked at Brock. "He wanted us to find her."

"Yeah." Brock nodded as he gently squeezed her hand. "Now that we know he's connected, we're searching into Collins's past. We'll find this guy, one way or another. They were connected. We've got him now. It's only a matter of time before we catch up to him."

She glanced around the tropical paradise. She could hear the sound of the guests playing in the pool a few feet away, just on the other side of the wall of palm leaves and flowers that she'd planted herself last year.

"What happens now?" she asked.

"Now?" He thought about it for a moment. "Now, we wait and lock down as much security as we can." He nodded towards the pool area. "It would help if we cancelled the rentals and had the place sit empty. But since I know that's not a possibility..."

"I'd go stir crazy," she admitted.

"Yeah." He smiled at her. "I get that. So we're vetting all the guests who are currently signed up to rent the place. I'll be sticking around here for as long as needed."

Just hearing that made her relax. "Thank you," she said softly. "I remember you, by the way." She glanced up at him. She needed him to know that, for some reason. It was important to her.

In the past two years, she'd gotten excited to find any articles or news about him. At first, there had been plenty. Then the articles on him had slowed down, much like the ones on her.

She'd even saved a few clippings, the ones where he'd been painted as her hero. Her rescuer. Because that's how she thought of him. He was the first face she saw. The first ray of light after a lifetime of darkness.

She knew that she'd somewhat built him up in her mind in the last two years. But in the past few days, he'd done nothing but prove those thoughts valid. He was her hero in every sense.

"You do?" he asked her, his eyes searching her face.

She nodded slightly. "For a while there, so many of my memories were blocked. Except seeing you hovering over me, promising me that I was safe. That from now on you'd make sure I was safe." She looked down at their joined hands. "It was that promise that kept me going."

"Crissy," he started, but then a loud burst of laughter from the pool area broke in and he stopped talking. Instead of continuing, he sighed and shook his head. "How about I give you a hand with whatever you have left on your list today?"

"That would be great." She stood up when he did.

"Would you like me to ask you every time I want to kiss you?" he said, and she realized just how closely they were standing.

"You don't have to," she assured him as she leaned up on her toes and brushed her lips across his.

"Good." He pulled her closer and deepened the kiss. She could just lose herself right there in his arms. Forget that the entire world existed. Forget that there were people just feet away from them. And most importantly, forget her past.

His lips and the taste of him were the sweetest nectar with the power to mesmerize. The feeling of his hands on her hips, slowly pulling her even closer to his hard body, caused her entire core to vibrate.

"Mama?" Emma's voice broke into the trance.

Crissy jerked away and took a step back. Her daughter stood in the doorway, rubbing her eyes while holding her favorite stuffed dog, Bruno.

"Hey, sweetie, did you have a good nap?" She walked over and picked Emma up.

"You were kissing Brock," Emma said clearly, causing Brock to laugh.

"I was," she said and stepped back inside.

"Why?" Emma asked.

"Because I wanted to," she answered easily as Brock followed them inside.

Emma was quiet for a moment. "Did he want to?"

"Yes, I did," he answered from behind them.

"How about we spend some time drawing?" she asked after getting her daughter a drink of water.

Emma pouted. "Can I kiss Brock?"

Brock laughed again. "If you want to." He easily walked over and took her daughter from her arms. Emma puckered her lips and placed them on his cheek. Then she frowned. "You're scratchy."

He reached up with his free hand and rubbed his short beard. "So, I am. Sorry, did I hurt you?"

"No, just tickled." Emma started to wiggle free from his arms. "I guess Mama likes the kissing part better." Brock easily set her down and laughed while Emma walked over to the arts cabinet and started getting out her coloring books and crayons.

"I guess my kisses aren't for everyone," he joked as he looked at Crissy.

"I guess not." She walked over and laid a hand on his face. "I like the beard," she assured him. "And the kissing part."

Brock's arms wrapped around her again, and she relaxed for just a moment, letting the worries about another killer out there waiting to get to her disappear.

At least for a moment. Then her phone rang, and she jumped in his arms.

"I'll answer it," he said, taking her shoulders.

"No." She took a deep breath. "I won't let him scare me from living. Besides, it's my job." She walked over to answer the call. Thankfully, it was from a woman looking to book the rental.

When she hung up from the call, Brock was sitting beside Emma, coloring with her.

"Wow, the two of you are so good at that," she said with a smile.

"You paint." Emma motioned to the cupboard.

She glanced down at her watch and winced. "I still have a few things to do."

"I can help," Brock said, starting to stand up.

"No, you stay here with her." She motioned to Emma, who had already turned back to her coloring. "I'll finish up quickly and be back to start dinner soon."

"Pizza!" Emma shouted.

She thought about it for a moment and asked Brock, "If you want? Eddie's is just down the street."

"Eddie's sounds good." He nodded. "I used to work there in high school."

"You did?" Emma stopped coloring and looked at him, as if suddenly he was the man of her dreams. "For real?"

"Yup," Brock said and started answering her daughter's million questions about working in her favorite pizza place.

She stepped back outside, and as Brock and her daughter's voices faded, the worry built. Worry about what would happen to Emma if anything happened to her.

Carl wasn't an option. Carl's parents were both deceased. He had a grandmother somewhere in a nursing home living off her government pension. Her father wasn't an option either. Nor did she want Emma to go into the system.

She thought of Brock and his parents. What it must have been like growing up in a loving home. What could she have become if she'd been nurtured in childhood? If she hadn't been afraid every moment of her life of being beaten or worse.

It was one thing Dr. Rizzo was helping her through now. Not letting fear ruin her life or stop her from living. The old Crissy would have never allowed Brock to kiss her. Would have never stepped out in the red swimsuit and been so carefree. Not after what she'd gone through.

For a while there, she'd been perfectly content spending the rest of her days hiding. Never taking any sort of pleasure for herself ever again.

Then something changed. She'd grown. Morphed into something new. And it was largely due to Emma and Dr. Rizzo's help.

The moment her daughter started forming sentences and was able to really interact with her, she'd started looking at life through Emma's eyes. Things could be amazing and fun, no matter the circumstances.

Somehow, she was having a difficult time returning to that line of belief after last night's call. Especially now, knowing that there was a woman out there that had hadn't been as lucky as she'd been two years ago.

She was just finishing up her chore list when Beth came through the fence. When she spotted Crissy carrying a basket of pool toys back to the large container they were housed in, she rushed over to her.

"Is it true?" Beth asked her a little breathless.

"Is what true?" she asked her.

"That the serial rapist and killer that kidnapped you is still out there?"

"I..." Crissy frowned. "We're not sure."

"It was all over the news," Beth said quickly. "You don't think he's coming for you here?" Beth glanced around.

"I..." Crissy didn't know what to say. Yes. Yes, she did

think he'd come for her. But she was confident that the police would find him first.

Beth shook her head. "I... I can't imagine what you've been through. How afraid you must be now." Beth wrapped her arms around Crissy. "We're here for you. If you need to stay with us, until..." Her friend's words dropped away as she looked over her shoulder.

Brock was walking towards them, holding a giggling Emma.

"Beth, this is..." She didn't get any further in her introduction. Beth rushed across the patio and hugged Brock.

"I didn't know you were back," Beth said cheerfully. "Oh, this makes things much better."

"I take it the two of you know each other?" Crissy said, taking Emma from Brock's arms.

"Yes, we went to school together," Beth answered.

"We went to prom together too," Brock said. "I was all set to marry you, then you fell for Oliver."

"He was a better cook than you," Beth joked. "Are you staying with Crissy and Emma?"

"Yeah," Brock said, nodding slightly towards Emma.

"That's good." Beth sighed heavily. "Very good. Now I don't have to worry so much."

"We were going to head to Eddie's for some pizza. Why don't you, Johnathan, and Tilly come with us?" Crissy asked.

Beth glanced between the trio. "That sounds great. I can see if Oliver can sneak away for dinner. He'd love to catch up with you," she said to Brock.

"Great." Brock smiled. "I can drive?"

"No," Beth and Crissy said at the same time.

"Parking is a headache. We can walk. It's only a block away," Beth answered.

"We'll leave in fifteen then," Crissy added. "I need to freshen up."

"Sounds good. I'll go get Johnathan, Tilly and myself ready." Beth turned to go. "Given the circumstances, I'm really happy you're here, Brock," she added before turning and rushing back through the fence.

"I didn't know Beth and Oliver were Tilly's parents," he said softly. "I guess I didn't put two and two together. I knew they'd had a kid."

"Two now," Crissy corrected.

"Right, and I'd heard they'd moved in next door, but…" He shrugged. "I guess I just wasn't thinking."

She carted Emma back inside and set her daughter down on the sofa. "Just how serious were you two?" she asked with a smile. "Should I be worried?"

He shook his head and smiled. "No, it was a million years ago. Besides, she and Ollie belonged together."

She nodded. "I'm going to go change." She glanced down at her work shorts and tank top. "Emma, why don't you go on up and put on those new shorts and the pink blouse I bought you last week?"

"Okay." Emma jumped up from the sofa, then turned to Brock. "Are you going to change too?"

He glanced down at his board shorts and T-shirt, then nodded. "Yeah, I suppose I will."

# CHAPTER TEN

The walk to the pizzeria was pleasant. The girls liked to ride in the wagon, so Brock pulled it behind them with both little girls cheering him on. Crissy and Beth walked together while Beth pushed Johnathan, who looked so much like Ollie, in a stroller.

He'd liked spending time with Emma, coloring and then reading a book to her. He had to admit, not having a television to be distracted by was good for the little girl. She played very well on her own and seemed to not need to be entertained like his nieces did. His mother assured him that the more kids his sister had, the more demanding they would be.

Still, part of him wished for a sibling for Emma. Seeing her interact with Tilly only confirmed that the little girl would enjoy having someone else to play with all of the time.

He'd always thought that he'd have a handful of kids himself. He remembered thinking how those kids would be blond-haired with blue eyes that matched Reagan's.

Emma was the spitting image of Crissy, except for the short hair. Emma's hair was shoulder length and always braided or put up in cute little pigtails.

Eddie's was a local place. Most tourists didn't know about the pizzeria, which sat off the back of the big market building. It was easily the best pizza in the Keys.

The place was surrounded by high-dollar restaurants that filled to the brim with sunburned tourists toting their screaming kids or college-aged singles partying it up.

Emma and Tilly sat quietly coloring the menu while they waited for their orders.

Before they had even sat down, he'd run into four other locals he knew. By the time their pizzas arrived, more than a dozen people had stopped to say hello to him.

"Wow, I guess you were pretty popular in school," Crissy said as she cut up Emma's pizza slice.

"Brock was prom-king popular," Beth chimed in as she shifted a sleepy Johnathan in her arms.

"You were queen," he reminded her.

"I was," Beth replied with a huge smile. "What about you?" Beth turned to Crissy. "I never asked where you grew up?"

He watched Crissy struggle with keeping the cheer in her eyes as she answered. "Here and there. Mainly just outside of Miami."

Beth narrowed her eyes slightly. "Your father is still alive, correct?"

"Yes." Crissy nodded. "Although I don't see or talk to him."

"Yeah, my father is a recovering drug addict. That's actually how Brock and I met. His father arrested mine in middle school. I had to show up at the station and post bail," Beth answered.

"You posted bail for your father when you were in middle school?" Crissy asked, looking surprised.

"Yes." Beth sighed. "Back then he used to get into all sorts of trouble. Reggie helped clean him up. By the time we hit high school, dad was clean and clear. Still is," she said with a smile. "My mother, on the other hand, took off. She's in Arizona somewhere with a new family." She shrugged.

"Oh, my mother left shortly after I was born. I guess the one positive thing about my dad was that he didn't give me up. Then again, I might have had a better go at childhood if he had," Crissy said. He noticed that the entire time she talked, she'd kept her eyes on her daughter to make sure the girls were too busy eating to pay attention to the adult conversation.

"Have you ever thought of tracking her down?" Beth asked Crissy.

He was thankful that Beth had agreed to tag along. She was asking Crissy all the things he'd wanted to ask her, plus some things he hadn't thought of.

So far, during the search, the police had yet to find anything on Crissy's mother. Short of a name, Emeline Jane Reeves, the woman seemed to have never existed.

"No," Crissy said with a frown. "Well, when I was younger. Any time I asked my father for a photo or her name, he'd... get angry. I learned to leave it alone."

"You don't even know her name?" Beth asked.

Crissy glanced at him. "I didn't. Not until recently."

He understood that she must have heard it from one of the many reports. Personal police files on both him and Crissy had been leaked to the press.

"What about now?" Beth asked between bites.

"Now?" Crissy shrugged. "I'm happier not knowing. If the woman wanted to meet me, it's not like I can't be found.

Everyone who watches or reads the news knows where I am."

When Ollie walked in and sat next to his family, the conversation turned to happier topics.

Oliver's family had moved to the Keys long before Brock's had. Brock and Ollie had filled the top spots in all the sports and social clubs. Between the pair of them, they'd earned most of the medals and awards at school.

Ollie was easily the happiest person Brock had ever met. The man constantly laughed and joked about everything.

It had been no surprise to anyone that he'd taken over his father's famous restaurant, named after him, his one and only son.

"How's the business going, Ollie?" Brock asked as he shook the man's hand after he'd given his daughter a hug and his wife and son a kiss.

"Great. How's the cop life?" Ollie asked.

Brock smiled. "Great."

"I heard you were taking a little sabbatical. Your parents were in my place last night," Ollie said.

"Yeah, I'm not sure you can call it a sabbatical, but it beats driving around Miami and dealing with drug busts and traffic stops."

He had an enjoyable time catching up with his old friend while Crissy and Beth chatted and kept the kids entertained.

Ollie had to leave and head back to work shortly after downing a slice of pizza.

"He normally gets more time with us, but they're short a few kitchen staff right now," Beth explained as they walked back home.

He stopped when they passed the center of the market.

"I bet you could sell your paintings here," he told Crissy, motioning to the art supply store. In the large glass window hung more than a dozen large paintings, all claiming to be from local artists.

"This is where Mama gets her paints," Emma chimed in.

The store was currently closed, but the lights in the windows highlighted local art for sale.

"I..." Crissy started.

"You paint?" Beth asked.

"Just as a hobby," Crissy said as her cheeks turned slightly pink.

He hadn't meant to embarrass her, but it had just come out when he'd seen the sign touting the local artists.

"I know Carrie, the owner of the store. We went to school with her daughter Lisa," Beth said. "If you want, I can put in a good word for you?"

"No, that's..." Crissy started to say, but then she looked at him.

"They're really good. Who knows, maybe you'll make enough to pay for some bigger canvasses or more paint supplies?" He shrugged.

"Okay," Crissy said with a nervous laugh.

"Great." Beth took Crissy's arm and started walking again. "I can't wait to see what you've painted."

He followed the pair, pulling the wagon behind him. By the time they made it back to the house, both girls and the little boy were fast asleep.

"They look so cute snuggled together," Beth said easily. "Why don't you let Emma spend the night?"

He could tell Crissy was about to deny her, but then she nodded. "Okay."

"I'll carry Tilly in, you get Emma," Beth told him as she set Johnathan's stroller just inside the door.

He easily lifted the sleeping girl in his arms and followed Beth inside the home. The place had been remodeled when he and his dad had been building the rental property. He could see the last owners had done a fine job as he weaved his way into the little girl's bedroom and gently set Emma down next to Tilly on the little girl's bed.

"I'll let Emma borrow some PJ's. Go on," Beth said, motioning to the door. "Go have some adult fun. God knows you both need it."

"What?" he asked her.

Beth rolled her eyes. "Everyone in the pizzeria could see it, the way the two of you were drooling over one another all night."

"I... we..." He thought of denying it, but then smirked. "Thanks." He quickly kissed Beth on the cheek and rushed back outside to where Crissy was putting the wagon away beside the walkway to the pool house.

Without giving her a chance to say anything, he pulled her into his arms and kissed her. He felt her relax against his chest as he walked them to the door of the pool house.

She fumbled with the lock, and they practically fell inside, laughing.

"You'll tell me if I go too fast?" he asked her as she pulled his button-up shirt off his shoulders.

"Yes," she agreed, and then she bent down and licked his shoulder before biting it softly. "You taste even better than you look," she moaned softly. "Put your hands on me." She covered his hands and moved them up to her breasts. Another moan escaped her lips, and he felt his entire body go hard.

"God," he said before covering her lips again.

"I want you inside me," she said against his mouth.

"Yes, soon." He bent down to run his mouth down her neck. He trailed his tongue over her soft skin, lapping up her scent as he played with her tight nipples through the soft cotton blouse she wore.

Instead of pulling it off her, he gently pulled it up until he'd exposed her belly. There he ran his fingers over the hem of the cotton skirt that she was wearing. When she wrapped her leg around his and pushed her body against him, he figured he had to change something or his time with her would be over far too fast.

He stepped back, and her eyes went wide when he dropped to his knees in front of her. Lifting the skirt, he kept his eyes locked with hers as he slowly ran his hands up her legs.

"You're so soft," he said, enjoying the feeling of her long legs in his hands. He couldn't remember wanting someone so bad before. Sure, it had been a while since he'd been with anyone, but he'd had dry spells before. This was different. Being with her was... different. "So... smooth," he added with a smile. She rolled her head back against the door and sighed.

"Oh god," she said when he ran a finger slowly over her silk underwear.

"Do you like that?" he asked. When she nodded, he said, "Tell me what you want."

"I want to feel your skin against mine," she said easily. "I want to feel you inside me."

"My fingers?" he asked, watching her face.

"Your fingers. Your tongue. Your dick." She shifted until her legs were a little wider.

He smiled. "In that order?"

She opened her eyes and looked down at him. "Yes," she said softly as he slipped a finger under the silk barrier between them.

# CHAPTER ELEVEN

Crissy tried to hold it together. With Brock's fingers rubbing her clit outside her silk panties, she knew that it would be a matter of seconds before she exploded.

After all, hadn't this been building for a while? She was like a volcano, ready to burst. Then he slid a finger over her skin, and she couldn't help but bite her bottom lip and wait for him.

"Tell me," he said again.

"I... please, Brock. I need a release," she begged, her fingers digging into his hair as he hovered between her thighs.

His finger slid inside her first, and she thought for sure that she was going to burst, but then his tongue lapped at her clit and everything that she'd been holding inside, that she'd kept locked away for years, rushed forth. She cried out his name as her body writhed and vibrated with the release.

"My god, Crissy." Brock's voice shook her moments later, and she realized he was carrying her. When he laid her down on her bed, she pulled him down on top of him.

"More. Again," she said, kissing him.

He covered her body, resting between her opened thighs. She felt him rubbing his hard dick against the outside of her panties.

"Why are there still so many barriers?" she asked, trying to pull his cotton shorts off his hips.

He pulled away and she removed her skirt and panties while he undressed. When he came back to her, they were skin to skin except for the rubber she'd watched him slide on.

This is what she wanted, what she needed, but when he got closer to her, the scent of the rubber hit her nostrils. The slightest smell of it caused the memory to surface. She was back in the container, tied up, blindfolded, and a victim once more. Instantly, her stomach lurched.

"Oh god!" she cried out. She pushed Brock aside as she rushed to the bathroom and lost her entire dinner.

"Hey." Brock was there, rubbing her shoulders.

"It's... not you," she said as tears rolled out of the corners of her eyes. "I swear."

He handed her a wet washcloth and slipped her robe over her shoulders.

"I know," he said gently.

"It's... the rubber. The smell of it." She closed her eyes. "I... he used it."

"Who?" he asked as she sat down on the bathroom floor.

He was sitting on the side of her bathtub, wearing only his boxer shorts.

"Not Collins," she said as she tucked her knees up to her chest and buried her face in her hands.

The fact that she could use that monster's name told her she no longer feared the man.

Then she realized that Brock was quiet. So quiet that

she glanced up at him. He was frowning down at the small package he'd pulled the rubber from.

"This brand?" he asked her, holding the foil package far enough away that she couldn't smell it, only see it.

"I... I'm not sure. It might be the same. The scent... it smelled the same."

"I'll look into getting a brand without a scent," he said as he set the package down on her bathroom sink.

"Thank you," she said, holding her head up. "I swear, it wasn't you."

"I know," he said, pulling her to her feet and wrapping his arms around her. She felt him kiss the top of her head as more tears seeped from her eyes. "Come on, let's go to bed."

"I... need a moment," she said as she dropped her arms from around his waist.

"Sure." He smiled at her, then turned and walked out of the bathroom.

Leaning against the sink, she looked deep into her own eyes and assured herself that she was once more safe. That it was in her past. That Brock was not mad at her or upset like Carl would have been.

After brushing her teeth and washing her face, she stepped back into her bedroom to find Brock sitting up in her bed.

"If it's okay, I'd like to sleep in here with you tonight," he said, pushing aside the blankets.

She easily walked over and slid under them and crawled into his arms.

"Yes," she said with a sigh. "It's okay."

"See, no weirdness." He kissed the top of her head.

"Thank you." She listened to his heart beating against her ear.

"No, thank *you*. You're amazing, by the way," he said,

and the sound of his voice vibrating in his chest soothed her further.

"Hm?" she asked.

"Seeing you come. Watching you let everything go." He sighed. "Amazing. I can't wait to see it again."

"Okay," she said and quickly fell asleep.

When she woke, she could hear Brock in the other room talking to her daughter. When she rolled over and saw the late hour, she almost sprinted out of bed.

She dressed quickly and rushed into the other room.

"How is it eight o'clock already?" she said, finger combing her hair away from her forehead.

"Well." Brock turned to smile at her. "It's easy. When the clock's little hand moves to the eight... and the big one goes all the way around and meets up with the twelve."

She rolled her eyes. Then he walked over and kissed her.

"Brock made breakfast!" Emma cheered.

"You're home." Crissy walked over and kissed her daughter on the top of her head, sniffing her hair. "And you're clean."

Emma giggled and wiggled away as Crissy tickled her daughter.

"Tilly and I took a bath. Then they brought me home. Now Brock is making me eggs and French toast." Emma reached up and took Crissy's face in her hands. "You need a bath."

Crissy frowned. "I do, but there's a lot of work..."

Her daughter had her laughing when she raised her eyebrows and pointed back to Crissy's room. "Bath. Now."

It was a line Crissy said all the time to her daughter when she complained about bath time.

"Go on. Shower." Brock nodded to the back of the house. "This'll be done in about ten. You've got time."

"Okay." She turned to go. "Do I smell that bad?" she asked Emma.

"Bath." Her daughter waved her off, and she laughed as she disappeared down the hallway.

After a quick shower, she pulled on some fresh clothes and was just about to step out into the living room when her phone rang. Somehow, she knew before she answered it that it was him.

"Did you get the message I left for you?" She didn't respond. Instead, she looked towards the door as Brock appeared. The look on his face told her that he understood who it was. He moved over to stand beside her. "There's another one coming soon. Just need to finish her up. Maybe tonight. God, I get so hard thinking about it." He chuckled. "I'll leave you a little something that'll remind you of our time together. Soon. I'm coming for you," he said before hanging up.

Crissy sat on the side of the bed when her legs folded under her.

Brock's phone rang almost instantly. He answered it and she half-listened to his one-sided conversation.

"Yeah, okay," he said finally. He hung up, and then he was holding her. "I've got you."

"I'm okay," she said several times. She shook her head and wiped her cheeks dry. "Breakfast," she said with a grin.

"It's ready," he assured her. "Are you..."

"I'm fine," she said after taking a deep breath. She had to be. Her daughter was waiting for her. "Let's go enjoy breakfast," she said, and he nodded and took her hand. She stopped him just inside the door. "Tell me they're going to get him."

"We're going to get him. I promise you. He will never lay a finger on you." He kissed her.

She smiled and already felt a little steadier as they walked out into the kitchen together. When she laid eyes on her daughter, however, a new possibility flooded her mind.

Brock must have sensed her fears about Emma instantly. He reached over and took her hand as he leaned closer.

"He won't even get near her. I promise you that on my life," he said in a low voice.

That promise echoed in her head for the entire day as she worked around the place, cleaning and helping the guests. Brock convinced her to take a few of her paintings down to the art store during lunchtime. The three of them ate at a burger place right in the harbor by the market.

Just sitting there watching the boats come and go, seeing the seagulls and pelicans floating overhead, she felt instantly better.

She was no longer surprised when someone stopped to chat with Brock. It really seemed as if he knew every single local on the island. More importantly, everyone seemed to like him and his family.

In the year that she'd lived there, she'd pretty much kept to the rental and to herself. She didn't even know the name of the woman in the grocery store she frequented twice a week.

Outside of Beth, Oliver, Tilly, Johnathan, Dr. Rizzo, and Brock's parents, she didn't know any other locals by name. Sure, she waved at the people who sat on their front porches as she walked around. In her mind, she'd made up names and stories for each face.

Not once had she actually stopped to chat or introduce herself to anyone. She hadn't thought to or needed to.

It was as if this was her first time talking with the owner of the store she'd been in more than a dozen times to purchase supplies. However, this was the first time Brock was with her and the first time she'd brought her art to show the older woman.

To say she was nervous would have been a complete understatement. Her hands shook, her palms were sweaty, and she even caught herself stuttering when she talked about her paintings.

Thankfully, Brock knew the woman well and covered for her. When they walked out of the store, she was minus all the pieces that she'd brought. And she had a promise from the woman that they would be highlighted in the window first thing the following morning.

"That went well," Brock said, taking her hand.

"I was a nervous wreck," she admitted, causing him to laugh.

"You were perfect. Artists are always nervous about showing their work." He wrapped his arm around her shoulder.

"They are?" She glanced at him. "What other artists do you know?"

"My mother," he explained quickly. "All the pieces in their house are hers. She sells them in a studio on the other side of the island."

"She does?" Crissy stopped and looked at him. "I didn't know that."

He smiled down at her and placed his hands on her shoulders. "That's because the two of you are a lot alike in that sense. You both hate talking about and showing off your talents." He bent down and kissed her on the nose. "Now come on. I think it's past Emma's nap time." He motioned to the wagon where her daughter was fast asleep under the little umbrella that kept the direct sunlight off her flawless skin.

# CHAPTER TWELVE

He'd carried Emma upstairs and tried to lay her on her bed without disturbing her, but the little girl had woken up. Then she'd convinced him to lie down with her by pouting. He'd meant to only lie there until she'd fallen back to sleep, but somehow had woken up almost an hour later when Crissy sat on the side of the bed.

"Did you have a good nap?" she asked softly.

"Hm?" He ran his hands over his face and then glanced at his clock. "Dang. I only meant to lie down for a second." He glanced around. "Where's Emma?"

Crissy smiled. "Downstairs, playing with her toys. She didn't want to wake you."

He rolled his shoulders. "I guess I was tired. How do you do it every day?"

"A lot of caffeine helps," she joked. "We were going to go for a swim. Do you want to join us?"

"Yeah." He thought about the calls he'd wanted to make after the little girl had gone down and when Crissy had been busy. They'd have to wait until later that evening when he could be alone.

Instead, he followed them outside and, for the next hour, played with Emma and Crissy in the pool.

The guests had gone off shopping or to explore the island and probably wouldn't be back until later that night, which gave them plenty of time to enjoy the pool and even grill and eat dinner outside.

"How about we watch a movie?" he suggested when the sun was setting, and they heard the guests had returned.

"Yes!" Emma shouted, but Crissy gave him a look that said she wasn't too sure.

"It's a cartoon movie. My sister's kids watch it all the time. I have a copy downloaded on my computer just in case they get bored when I visit."

"Please?" Emma started as she climbed up on Crissy's lap.

"Fine." Crissy smiled down at her daughter. "But you have to take a bath and get your pajamas on first."

"I'll even brush my teeth." The little girl jumped off Crissy's lap.

"You can skip that until later. I'm going to make us some popcorn," Crissy said, causing Emma to cheer again as she rushed up the stairs. "Thank you." Crissy turned to him.

"I should have cleared it with you first," he admitted.

"No, it's okay. Sometimes I forget to step outside my comfort zone." Her eyes turned towards the stairs. "It's easy to forget that there is a lot in life Emma hasn't experienced yet."

He thought about what it would be like to fall into a pattern of life like that. Then he realized he'd done just that in Miami. Hadn't the last few years bled into one another?

As he helped her make the snacks, he thought about what his life would be like here, with Crissy and Emma.

He'd left the Keys because he'd been searching for

excitement. He hadn't wanted to fall into the grind of daily life. Yet, after a while, it had still found him.

Sure, there was plenty of excitement as far as his job went. Not a day went by where he wasn't running after some strung-out druggy or chasing down a drunk driver. Looking at it now, he realized that wasn't the kind of excitement he wanted any longer.

Watching Emma sing and dance along to the music from the movie was more fun than he could remember having in a long time. The moment the movie was over, she begged to watch it again, but Crissy reminded her that it was already ten minutes past her bedtime.

"Book. Book," Emma cheered.

"Okay, one story," Crissy agreed. She started walking Emma up the narrow stairs.

"No, Brock." Emma turned and held out her little hand for his.

Crissy looked at him, her eyebrows raised slightly. "I think Brock needs to get some work done."

Emma started pouting, and his heart melted.

"One story," he agreed. "If it's okay with your mom."

Crissy nodded, and he followed them up the stairs.

He was surprised at the collection of classic books on the little girl's bookshelf. His nieces had all the latest Disney stories. Books that sang or talked or even had popup pictures. Emma's were all older and some were even missing a few pages.

"You need some new books," he said as she looked through the small shelf trying to find the one that she wanted him to read.

"Mama says I'll get some on my birthday," Emma replied.

"Oh yeah?" he asked as she picked out *The Princess and*

*the Pea*, which had obviously been read too many times. The cover was faded, and the pages were so thin, he worried he'd tear them.

The little girl fell asleep before the end of the story, leaving him and Crissy tiptoeing down the stairs.

"Thank you," Crissy said softly at the base of the stairs.

"For?"

"For tonight," she replied, smiling.

"When is Emma's birthday?" he asked, curious.

"Next month on the tenth."

"No way." He smiled. "Mine's on the tenth of June too."

"Seriously?" she asked with a slight frown. "How did I not know that?"

His smile grew. "Why would you?" He moved closer to her and watched her cheeks turn slightly pink. "Have you been looking into me?"

"Maybe," she said slowly. "I bet you know all sorts of things about me. From the police files."

"Well"—his hands moved to her hips— "you'd be right. For example. I know that your birthday is January second."

She stilled in his arms. "No, it's not."

He chuckled, then frowned. "That's what your birth certificate says."

"My birthday is in August," she said, shaking her head.

He tilted his head and tried to pull up the image of the certificate in his mind. "Your birth certificate on file says January second. I'm sure of it."

She stepped back out of his hands. "Show me."

He thought of all the trouble he could get into for showing her anything from her sealed file, then he shrugged those fears off and walked over to open his laptop.

After opening her file, he showed her the copy of her

birth certificate on file with the state. "I was right, January second."

She leaned closer and scanned the file. "This isn't mine." She waved her hand. Then she stood up, disappeared into the back, and a few short seconds later came back carrying a piece of paper. "This is mine. See, August eighteenth."

He held up the document next to his screen. They were identical except for the date and the fact that her mother's name was missing on her copy. "Your copy doesn't even have your mother's name."

"My dad said he erased it after she took off." Crissy shrugged. "Still, I've never needed to show it to anyone so…"

He examined the copy in his hands a little closer and instantly knew that it was fake. Which made him wonder if the one the police had scanned and put in her file was fake too.

"These are fake," he said to himself.

"What?" Crissy jerked next to him.

"This one for sure." He showed her the paper. "There's supposed to be a state seal here." He ran his fingers over the spot where the paper was flat. "I can't tell on this scanned one if the seal is there." He zoomed the image in, but it was too fuzzy to tell. "I can request a copy of it to make sure."

"Why would my dad have a fake birth certificate for me?" she asked.

He spoke without thinking and instantly wished he hadn't. "Maybe he's not really your dad?" Crissy slouched next to him, and he had to reach around and hold onto her. "Hey," he said, pulling her closer. "It was just a thought."

"I…" She shook her head. "How can we find out for sure?"

"Did they fingerprint you?" he asked after thinking for a moment. "When they found you?"

She thought about it for a moment, then shook her head. "Why would my fingerprints be linked to anyone other than me?"

"Okay, so you said your mom took off shortly after you were born. What's the earliest memory you have?" he asked her.

She shifted on the sofa slightly and was quiet for a moment. "I had a friend."

"Name?"

"Jade," she said with a smile. "She was my best friend. We did everything together. I used to ask my dad about her all the time, and he would tell me she was made up." Crissy frowned. "Then later, when I'd ask about her, he'd slap me." She shrugged. "So I stopped asking."

"Jade?" he said with a frown. "That's a pretty unusual made-up name for a fake friend. How old were you?"

"Maybe three or four?" She shrugged. "It's why it's important that I give Emma happiness at this point in her life. Soon, she'll be making her first memories."

His heart did a little happy twist at that thought. How cool must it be for a parent to mold their kids first memories?

"What about you?" She interrupted his thoughts.

"Hm?" he asked, focusing again.

"What's your first memory?" she asked.

He smiled. "Going down the water slide at the water park in Orlando. My folks took me to Disney for my fourth birthday. Besides a ton of pictures, none of which were of me on that slide, I remember so much of that trip."

"How wonderful. What a great first memory." She was quiet and he watched her eyes move up to the loft.

"Thinking of taking Emma there for her birthday?" he asked.

"I was." She sighed. "But I haven't managed to save up enough. Even with the discount they give for residents in the state." She sighed. "It's pretty expensive."

"Yeah." He thought about it, wondered, for the first time how much his parents were paying her. "You could always ask for a raise. I'm pretty sure your boss will give it to you, in light of... things."

"No." She smiled. "Your parents are paying me too much as it is." She leaned back.

Without thinking, he pulled her legs up onto his lap and started rubbing her calves. She was tense at first, but then relaxed.

"You're good at that," she said with a slight groan.

He smiled. "I dated a massage therapist once."

"Oh?" She arched her brows.

"Lisa. We saw each other for a few weeks. Then things fizzled out."

"What's the longest relationship you've been in?"

"Reagan. We dated for a year." He let his hands roam up to where her cotton shorts sat high on her thighs.

"Right." She sighed and shifted. "Don't stop." She closed her eyes. "Please."

His fingers slid higher, under the cotton. She was still wearing her swimsuit underneath the loose shorts. When he moved to pull the shorts off her hips, she arched and then kicked them to the floor.

She was wearing a sexy white two-piece swimsuit. The contrast between the white of the suit and the tan of her skin was intoxicating. He ran a finger over the mound the suit made over her pussy and smiled when she moaned his name.

"Are you going to come for me again, Crissy?" he asked in a low tone.

"Yes." She sighed and spread her legs a little wider. Then her eyes opened and focused on him. "This time, you'll come for me too."

He smiled and nodded. He'd stopped by the store and had purchased non-scented rubbers just for her.

He untied the sides of the strings that held her swimsuit bottoms together and pushed them aside, then he ran his eyes over her. She was still wearing a white tank top and the top to the swimsuit, but she looked so good. Too good. His eyes moved back to the neat little triangle of hair covering her sex.

"Perfection," he said softly. Then he leaned down and lapped at her, enjoying the taste of her on his tongue.

She wrapped her legs around his shoulders as her fingers slid into his hair.

"Brock," she moaned, then she made a sexy little high-pitched sound and convulsed around him.

He slid off his shorts and shirt, put on the rubber, then slowly went up her body, running his lips over her, nudging her tank top and bikini top off her until she lay under him, bare.

His hands roamed over her hips as he kissed her. "Tell me what you want," he said next to her ear.

"You. Please, I want to feel you inside me. I want to... enjoy," she said with a slight sigh.

He leaned back and looked down at her as he paused just outside her entrance, the head of his dick hugged by her pussy lips.

"Look at me," he said, needing to watch her feel him, watch pleasure spread on her face as he slowly entered her. Filled her.

Her short nails dug into his shoulders and her legs tightened around his hips. She arched back and closed her eyes again as he started rocking slowly. She felt so good. Better than he could remember ever feeling.

As he felt her convulse around him, he knew that he could easily stay right there inside her for the rest of his life.

# CHAPTER THIRTEEN

Crissy woke when Brock lifted her from the sofa into his arms.

"Shh," he said softly. "We're just going to head into the bedroom. I'd hate for Emma to wake and find us on the sofa," he said next to her ear.

"Mkay," she said and then yawned.

When Brock laid her down on the bed, she turned over, and a few seconds later she felt him climb in behind her and snuggle up against her back.

"Carl wasn't a snuggler," she said, not fully awake.

"No?" Brock asked. "Reagan hated it. She claimed I was always too warm."

"I like it." She sighed and scooted her butt up against him. She smiled when she felt him grow hard against her hip. "Now I really like it."

He chuckled. "Careful," he warned. "We might not get any sleep tonight if you keep that up."

"We can always take a nap tomorrow," she said and wiggled again.

She felt so good. So... sexual. Again. Finally, sex wasn't something she feared. She'd taken it back. Made it hers to enjoy once more.

The fear of the act had built in her head over the past two years of her celibacy. Having her last encounters be so scary, so full of fear, had done a number on her psyche. Tonight, she'd taken back that part of her life and it was all thanks to Brock.

Rolling over, she shifted until she sat over him. Feeling free of the burden, she rained tiny kisses over his face. She paused over his lips and kissed him as she grinded against his hardness. His hands moved up to her hair, holding her mouth against his for a moment.

Then she was trailing her mouth down his neck, slowly moving her way down his hard chest. She enjoyed sucking his flat nipples until they puckered for her. Then she moved on down that hard six-pack, ran over his bellybutton, and finally shifted down to rest between his thighs.

"Crissy?" Her name came out as a warning as she trailed the tip of her tongue over the head of his dick, which jumped at her slight touch.

Giggling, she wrapped her fingers around him and held him still as she enjoyed the taste of him. "I want to lap you up, like you did me. I want to taste you on my lips when I wake," she said just before she took him into her mouth.

His fingers tightened in her hair as he growled her name. She felt him growing harder in her mouth and was enjoying pleasing him for a moment. But then he sat up and his hands moved under her armpits as he hauled her back up to him. He nudged her legs aside and reached for a condom. He slid it on and then positioned her over him again.

"Ride me," he said, his eyes locked on her.

Smiling, she moved up to her knees. She lay her palms flat on his chest and held herself over him while he positioned his dick just outside her.

"Do it," he said, moving his hands aside.

When she slid down on him slowly, a tear of happiness slipped from her eyes. For the first time in two years, she finally felt completely free.

"Are you okay?" Brock asked her moments later when he pulled her against his chest tightly as their bodies cooled.

"Yes," she said with a smile. "You?"

"Perfect." He was quiet for a moment. "You were crying."

"Happy tears," she assured him. "I finally feel free." She shifted to look at him. "Part of me was still locked up in that container." She leaned down and kissed him. "You helped free it."

He lifted his hand and cupped her face. "You're so beautiful and amazing." He pulled her back down for another kiss.

She fell asleep wrapped in the arms of a man and, for the first time in two years, had only happy dreams.

The following day was yet again a perfect one. They woke and had breakfast together, then after she dropped Emma off next door, she rushed around and cleaned the rental while the guests were out at the beach for the day. Brock installed two new cameras and did a huge chunk of the items off her Crazy List.

Since they had the place to themselves for lunch, they spent it by the pool and playing in the water.

When Emma went down for a nap, she and Brock returned outside to enjoy some lazy time in the water.

She hadn't expected it when he pulled her up close

against him and started running his hands under her swimsuit. It was so easy to be with him.

So easy to lie back in the cool water and let him please her. To please him. Even though she knew she was pouring more of her feelings into her kisses, she kept denying that she'd fallen for him. Fallen hard.

She kept telling herself that he was only there temporarily. That he had a job in Miami to return to. A life. One that didn't include her and Emma.

Falling into a pattern of being around Brock was easy. They stole moments here and there during their day to kiss or please one another. After the pool, they lounged on the chairs in the sun. When Emma woke, they all sat down and colored while she waited for the laundry to finish.

Her daughter had grown so attached to Chester that she knew she would have to get a cat of their own when Brock left. She didn't want to think about him leaving, so she pushed that to the back of her mind.

Everything was just... normally perfect. She could almost forget there was someone after her. Almost forget the crazy world outside of their little paradise.

They had just finished dinner when there was a knock on the front door of the pool house. She never used that door. It was technically the front door, but she always thought of that part of the house as the back side, even though it faced a smaller street that was the legal address of the pool house.

"Are you expecting someone?" Brock asked her.

"No," she said, feeling her heart jump. "No one goes to that door." She walked over and laid a hand on Emma, who was sitting at the counter, playing with her toys.

"Stay put." Brock disappeared down the hallway. When he came back, she noticed the gun held by his side. "Take

Emma upstairs," he said. Crissy had already snatched up her daughter and was halfway up the stairs.

She listened to Brock ask who it was through the door, as she held her daughter tight to her chest.

"Delivery for... Crissy Talbot," she heard clearly.

"Just leave it there," Brock replied.

"I'm sorry, sir, I can't. She's being served legal papers," the voice called back clearly.

"Hold up your badge," Brock replied as he looked through the peephole. Then she heard Brock open the front door and greet the person. "Hell, Randy. I didn't know that was you."

"Brock?" the other voice said sounding surprised. "What are you doing here?"

"This is my folk's place," Brock said, then he called up to them, "We're clear. Come on down."

"Mama, you're squeezing me too tight?" Emma said, her voice sounding scared.

"Sorry, baby." Crissy relaxed her hold. "Shall we go downstairs and see who it is?"

There was a middle-aged man in a full police uniform standing in her living room and talking with Brock when they came downstairs.

"Crissy, this is Randy O'Hare. Randy, Crissy Talbot. And her daughter, Emma."

"Ma'am." Randy nodded. "Sorry to do this, but..." He handed her a thick envelope.

"Thanks," she said and frowned down at it. She half-listened to Brock and Randy catch up. Thankfully, less than five minutes after the man had walked into her home, he left.

"Well?" Brock said, turning to her after locking the front door. He nodded to the envelope.

She sat it down on the counter and picked up Emma. "Later," she said with a smile. "Time for bed."

Emma groaned, but then turned to Brock. "Story?"

"Sure, princess," Brock said. "Give me a minute," he told Emma, then he disappeared back down the hallway. When he returned, she knew that his weapon was put somewhere safe once again. Then he took Emma from her hands and disappeared upstairs, leaving her time to sit down and open the papers.

When Brock returned downstairs less than half an hour later, he sat next to her and took a sip of her wine.

"So?" he asked, pulling her into his arms.

"Carl is suing me for custody and alimony," she said dryly.

He sighed. "Yeah, I thought it might be something like that. I can have my dad send you his lawyers' info?"

She shifted closer to him. "Thanks. I just can't think about this right now."

"It does seem trivial when there's..." He dropped off.

"Someone out to kill me?" she finished for him.

"Yeah." He sighed, and she felt his arm tighten around her momentarily.

"Let's talk about my birth certificate," she said, suddenly sitting back up.

"Okay," he said slowly. He sat up as well.

"How would we get to the bottom of this?" she asked. She'd been thinking about it all day.

He stood up suddenly and grabbed his computer. "Well, I did a little research today." He set it down and turned it on. "There doesn't appear to have been an Emeline Jane Reeves or Emmaline Jane Reeves that lived in the state of Florida and had a daughter. So, I had a friend in the FBI widen the search."

"You have a friend in the FBI?"

He smiled. "A few."

"Okay, what did you find?" She looked at his screen.

"There are three that fit roughly the age requirements. None of them registered having girls though."

"Only three?" She frowned.

"One died when she was ten, long before you were born, and another died in a car accident a year before your birth. Which leaves us with..." He turned the screen around and showed her a picture of a black woman.

"This is the only one left?" she asked.

"Yup." His eyes ran over her.

"Brock." She shook her head. "I... this can't be right."

"It could be. Mixed race couples could have—"

"No, I get that, and it wouldn't bother me if that were true but... you don't understand. My father..." She felt her stomach roll. "My father is and always has been extremely racist. There is no way he would have been with this woman."

Brock frowned then sighed. "Okay, but it's worth a call, don't you think?"

She thought about what she would say to a stranger. Any stranger. Hey, did you have a baby girl twenty-eight years ago and leave her with a racist asshat who abused her almost every day of her life?

"Can you call?" She turned to him. "You know, since you're the police?"

He nodded and pulled out his phone and dialed the number. When he hung up without talking to anyone she asked, "What?"

"It's an invalid number." He tried once more. "Let me..." He typed and maneuvered to a different site, then dialed the phone again.

"Afternoon," he said into the phone, "is this Emeline Jane Reeves?" When she responded, he put the phone on speaker so she could hear both sides of the conversation. "This is officer Brock Miller with Key West PD. I'm doing an investigation into a Crissy Talbot, and I'm trying to track down her biological parents. Your name appears on her birth certificate. You wouldn't have happened to have a daughter on..."—he shrugged— "either January second or August eighteenth twenty-eight years ago, would you?"

"Wow, um, no. I've got two kids. I don't want any more." The woman chuckled. "What's this... Crissy Talbot done?"

"Oh, nothing herself. It's an ongoing case. She's the victim," he assured the woman.

"Hm, well..." There was a long pause. "I'm a circuit judge here in Miami-Dade County, which assures me, officer, that you used the official database to track down my private number."

Brock winced. "Yes, ma'am," he responded.

"The answer is no. I didn't have a child twenty-eight years ago. Both my boys are in their teens."

"Thank you, Judge." He started to reach over to hang up the phone, but Crissy stopped him.

"Judge?" Crissy asked. "This is Crissy. I wonder if I could ask you a question?"

There was another pause for a moment. "Shoot," the judge finally said.

"Did you ever prosecute a Simon Jones?" Crissy asked, holding her breath. Over the years, her father had adopted the names of lawyers or judges that had processed him. She'd grown up having dogs named after female officers that had arrested him. He used to call them all bitches regularly, as if it was a joke. They had even had a rooster named after his parole officer once. Her dad enjoyed eating that bird for dinner, even burned it extra crisp as he'd laughed over the fire.

"Simon Jones?" The judge sighed. "I never prosecuted him, but I was his court-appointed lawyer several times back some thirty years ago."

# CHAPTER FOURTEEN

Crissy looked over at Brock with a strange look in her eyes.

"What's Simon Jones got to do with..." Then she was quiet. "Did you say Crissy Talbot? As in, the survivor of those cop serial killers?"

"Yes, Judge," Brock answered.

"Oh, and you think Simon Jones has something to do with that case?" the judge asked.

"No, ma'am," Brock answered.

"He's my father," Crissy added.

There was a moment of silence before the woman burst out laughing. "I'm sorry, say that again?"

Crissy frowned over at Brock.

"Crissy Talbot is Simon Jones's daughter," Brock answered.

"And... on the birth certificate, it shows me as the mother?" she asked.

"Spelled differently on two different documents. It even shows two different birthdays," Brock answered.

"Shoot me a copy of both documents. Here's my email

address…" The woman gave him her email, and he sent digital copies of both birth certificates over to her. They waited as the judge received and opened the email. "That son of a…" she finally said with a sigh. "Both of those dates coincide with the cases I handled for him."

"What?" Crissy sat forward.

"You're sure?" Brock asked.

"Case number 9887450102, January second, and case number 9887450818, August eighteenth. Both of them were DUIs. Which is why they fell in my lap. He lost his license the first go-round. The second he was jailed for two years," the judge answered. "I can send the case numbers back to this email address."

"Thank you," Brock answered. "I'm sorry we took up your evening."

"It's no problem. I'm really sorry for what you went through Miss Talbot. I would have liked to have both of those scumbags that did that to you stand in front of me so I could have served you some justice."

"Thank you," Crissy said softly. "Judge?" Crissy asked. "Is there any way you can look at another case for me? My ex-husband is trying to get custody of my daughter. I thought the case was closed last year, but…"

"Shoot me the file number, I'll see what I can do and get back to you when I can." the judge said. "It's the least I can do for my daughter." She laughed as she hung up.

"That went better than expected," Brock said after he sent the new case number Crissy gave him.

"How?" Crissy frowned. "I just found out I have no mother."

He put his arms around her and held on. "On the bright side, there's a good possibility that Simon isn't your father."

She sighed. "I think I need to make a trip up north."

"Can't you call him?" Brock asked.

Crissy leaned back and looked at him with a shocked look on her face. "My father doesn't have one of those tracking devices you put in your pocket. After all, the government listens to everything you say and do," she said in a deep voice, no doubt mimicking her father's tone.

"Right." He nodded. "We can see if my mom can watch Emma for a day and drive up there together, if you'd like." He watched a variety of emotions cross her face as she thought about it.

"That would be wonderful. Emma likes your mom," Crissy answered.

"My mom loves Emma. I can tell." He pulled her back down. "Okay, so what did we find out?"

"I have no parents," she said against his chest. "Maybe I'm a test-tube baby?" she joked. "Immaculate conception... only I have a father?"

He laughed. "No, what we found out was your father didn't want anyone to know who your mother was." He frowned and realized what that usually meant.

"Which means?" she asked, looking up at him.

"Which means it was either someone underage, illegal, or..." He felt his stomach twist at the last possibility.

"Or?" Crissy asked.

"Or..." He looked down at her. "You're not his at all."

She frowned up at him, and he watched as she realized what it was that he was saying. She sat up slowly. "You think my father kidnapped me?"

Just then Brock's phone rang. Seeing his father's number on his screen gave him another sinking feeling.

"Evening," he answered.

"Evening," his dad said in a tone that assured Brock that he had bad news.

"They've identified the girl found in the warehouse. It wasn't the seventeen-year-old girl that went missing. It was a fifteen-year-old that had been reported as a runaway over a year ago," his dad said. "Which means that there's a good possibility that the seventeen-year-old will be our next find. I've sent you the file number. Son, there are some pretty bad photos in it. You'll want to shield Crissy from them."

"Will do," he agreed. Crissy was watching him like a hawk. "Anything else?"

"There are a lot of similarities. Either this guy had access to the scene of the crime or... he was in on it like you and Crissy claim. There are burn marks... everywhere on the body. Ones that match the photos of Crissy."

"Right." He sighed, feeling sick to his stomach. "We've got other news," he said and then quickly filled his dad in on the call with the judge.

"Damn, seriously?" his father said. "Okay, I know someone who might be able to help us search for Crissy's biological parents," his father surprised him by saying.

"How?" he asked.

"We've got her DNA on file. It's as easy as putting it in the right databases. I'll keep you posted on that."

DNA. Of course. In a case like Crissy's, they would have taken her DNA to compare her blood to the other blood that they'd found in that container.

Why hadn't Brock thought of that? So many people sent their spit in tubes to different companies to see where they'd come from. He hadn't needed to since his mother kept all their ancestry information in a large binder at home. He could trace both of his parents' lineages clear back to Ireland and England for a few generations.

"Thanks," Brock said and then asked about his mom watching Emma the following day so he and Crissy could head up to see her dad. Her mother happily agreed. He hung up and filled Crissy in on most of the conversation.

"Come on," he said once he was done. He took Crissy's hand, pulled her up, and walked her back to the bedroom. "Let's put this all away for the night." He kissed her.

"Oh?" She smiled up at him. "What were you thinking to take my mind off things?"

God, what was he going to do when he had to return home? Did he have to? Why? Those questions ran through his head as she fell asleep later in his arms.

When they woke the next morning, his mother arrived with fresh baked muffins and coffee. She was happily greeted by Emma, who instantly ignored both him and Crissy the entire time his mother was there.

A little over an hour later, he and Crissy left the Keys and headed up the state to where her father was living.

"What should I expect?" he asked her.

"I wish I knew," she admitted. "The last time I was at the house..." She shook her head. "Half of it had fallen in during the last hurricane."

"Is your dad a big gun owner?"

"What true conspiracy theorist isn't?" she said dryly.

"Okay, but at least he won't shoot at you, right?" he said, wishing for backup.

As an answer, she shrugged. "I'm not sure what state the man will be in. To be honest, after finding out what we have, everything I knew about the man is..." She made a motion with her hands as if she was blowing something up. "Poof," she added.

"Right. Okay, I've gone into lots of situations blind before." He thought back to when he'd walked into the storage container. He hadn't been expecting to find anyone. He'd simply been searching the property for any reason why his partner had kidnapped Emily Stokes and Jamie Garner. He'd hoped that he would find proof of his partner's innocence. Instead, he'd found Crissy.

He followed her directions and turned off the highway on an exit that had no amenities. The old highway bridge appeared as if it was ready to fall in on itself.

From there, they turned left and drove for about ten miles.

"Turn left here," she said, getting his attention.

He slowed down. "Where?"

"At the post." She motioned to a wood stake in the ground.

"Is there a road?"

"Not really," she answered as he turned. The tree branches scraped the side of his Jeep, and he silently calculated how much damage would be done to his paint job.

Then the dirt path opened up to a small clearing. There were two buildings sitting at the base of large mangroves right at the edge of swamp water. One building was up on old log stilts and the other, true to Crissy's word, was half destroyed and caving in on itself.

"It looks like he's been living in the shed." She motioned to the other building.

He glanced over in time to see a man standing on a small porch, pointing a shotgun at his Jeep.

"Daddy," Crissy called out after she rolled down the window. "It's me."

The shotgun lowered slightly as he parked.

"Here we go," she said with a sigh. He took her hand and squeezed it before shutting off the engine.

"I'm right here," he assured her.

She nodded and stepped out of the Jeep at the same time he did.

Thankfully, they made it to the steps without getting shot at.

"What're you doing here?" her father asked.

The man was slightly older and a great deal heavier than his last mug shot. It had been hard to tell in those pictures if Crissy had any resemblance to her father, but seeing them standing next to one another, he couldn't see any. Not that that was a clear sign, just another clue.

"Daddy, this is Brock Miller," Crissy said. "Can we come in?"

"What do you do for a living, boy?" her father asked, not moving from his spot.

The panicked look on Crissy's face told him instantly to lie.

"I'm in between jobs right now," he answered quickly.

Her father was quiet for a moment then nodded. "It's this damned economy. The damned government is sucking the common man dry." Her father set the shotgun down on the porch by a handmade rocking chair and then opened the screen door. There were more gaping holes in the screen than there was screen material.

He followed Crissy into the small ten-by-ten building. Inside, he was slightly surprised at how organized the place was, though it was filthy.

There was a small bed, a sofa, and what appeared to be a kitchen area.

"Did he knock you up like that last one did?" her father asked, getting his attention.

"No, daddy. I'm not pregnant," Crissy answered.

Her father glanced in his direction and then nodded. "At least he's an improvement over that last feller." He turned towards the kitchen and held up a jar full of brown liquid. "Want some tea?" her father asked them.

"No, thank you," Crissy said and then shook her head at him.

"No, thanks," he responded.

"Well, go ahead and sit down." Her father motioned to the sofa. He really didn't want to sit on the tattered sofa.

"Daddy," Crissy said, taking a step towards the older man, "did you steal me?"

He had to admit Crissy's fast approach did one thing in their favor. It surprised her father enough that the truth, no matter how quickly masked, flashed on the older man's face.

# CHAPTER FIFTEEN

Crissy noticed the look of guilt on her father's face instantly. It was the number one reason he hadn't been able to get away with anything in court. He had a shitty poker face.

"You did!" She took another step towards the man who had abused her all her life. What she wanted to do was beat the truth out of him. "From whom? Why?" She took another step forward.

She felt Brock's gentle hand on her shoulder but was too busy demanding answers to care.

"Answer me!" she screamed.

"I think it's time you left," her father said, taking Crissy's arm and moving to shove her towards the door.

Brock stepped forward and hovered over the man. "You don't get to touch her," Brock said in a low warning tone.

Her father turned to Brock, his face turning beet red. "You'd better back off, boy," her father said loudly. "This is my property."

"Is it? Legally?" Brock said in a calm tone as he stepped

between her and her father, forcing her dad to drop his hold on her.

"What do you want? A confession?" Her father turned on her. "Fine. I stole ya." He threw up his hands, pulled a bottle of moonshine from a tin can, and took a large swig.

She knew firsthand that he made the stuff himself. His still was probably not far from the hut he was calling home. When she'd been in middle school, she'd drank an entire jar of it in one sitting. She'd hoped to numb the pain after getting whooped with her father's belt. Instead, she'd passed out and fallen out of the tree she'd been hiding in. She'd ended up with a busted finger and a sprained wrist. Not to mention that she'd vomited all the next day. It was the number one reason she only drank wine and beer. She detested the taste of anything stronger.

"From whom?" she asked, feeling her chest tighten.

He didn't answer, but instead took several more swigs of the moonshine.

"Who?" She screamed it, the sound vibrating in the small space.

"That rich asshole who hired me and refused to pay me," her father said with a laugh as he took another swig.

"Who?" she asked, shaking her head.

"Oswald!" her father spat back. "He had two of ya. I figured he owed me. Then, when he refused to pay the ransom..." He shrugged.

Crissy felt the panic attack coming on and sat down on the soiled sofa, not caring if her jean shorts got dirty or stained at this point. Everything about her felt dirty, starting from the inside out.

"Oswald?" she asked with a shake of her head.

"Patrick Oswald. He hired me to do some work around

his big place, then refused to pay me what I was owed," her father said between swigs.

"Oswald," Crissy said several times, letting the name sink in. Then she replayed what her father had said. "He had two of us?" She glanced up and shook her head. "What does that mean?"

"Twins," Brock said, showing her his phone. While she'd been processing the information, he'd been searching the internet.

Sure enough, there was an old article about Patrick and Julia Oswald. One of their twin daughters had gone missing.

Crissy took the phone from his hand and looked at the two images. The first was a grainy picture of the family—a man and woman wearing all white and holding two identical daughters dressed in white sundresses. The other image was of just the twin girls. Underneath it said, "Amber and Jade Oswald, age four."

Jade. Jade. Her make-believe friend. Her eyes moved up to her father.

"You stole me," she said, standing up, feeling her anger grow. "You stole me!" she screamed.

When she lunged at her father, Brock was there, holding her back.

Her father—no, scratch that—Simon Jones, the man who had stolen her from her real family as a child, laughed at her as if he was enjoying her pain.

"Easy," Brock said next to her ear. "He's not worth it."

"He stole me," she said again as it sank in even more. Her entire body vibrated with anger. She shook with the knowledge that her entire life was a lie.

She had a twin. She had a family. One that, if she hadn't been stolen, would have loved her.

"And he'll rot in prison for it," Brock said easily.

"Like hell I will. I'd like to see the police get within ten feet of this place," Simon spat back as he took another swing of his moonshine.

Brock's hands shifted on her. Then he walked over and yanked her father's hands behind him. The bottle of moonshine fell to the floor, soiling the wood planks and shattering the glass. Brock slapped handcuffs on Simon, the move so quick that neither she nor Simon could react fast enough.

"Simon Jones, you're under arrest for the kidnapping of Amber Oswald. You have the right to remain silent..."

Crissy sat back down on the sofa as Brock read Simon his Miranda rights. Her head was spinning so fast, she felt light-headed. She was surprised to hear sirens approaching the property by the time he was done.

Simon was trying to jerk free of Brock's hold and cursing up a storm the entire time. The man who had abused her all of her life was yelling and screaming. His face was bright red as Brock held him firmly.

"When did you call the police?" she asked as he started walking Simon out the door.

"I pocket-dialed my dad when Simon started to confess. Then I searched the Oswalds as a distraction for time," Brock said. "My dad's got it all and sent local PD." He shoved the older man outside to the newly arrived police cruiser.

For the next half hour, she relayed what had happened in the shed. What Simon had said to her, what he'd confessed.

Then they'd climbed back in the Jeep as Simon was driven away.

"Are you okay?" Brock asked, but she shook her head

and just continued to breathe as he started driving. Instead of heading back down Highway One, Brock pulled off the highway and headed into Miami.

"Where are we going?" she asked.

"We'll have to sign some documents at the station. Also, if it's okay with you, we can spend the night at my place here. My mom can watch Emma for the night. I think you deserve a reprieve."

She didn't argue. Her head was still spinning. They parked at a police station's private lot just as they were hauling her father inside. Brock had used a code to get into the secure area.

"This is where you used to work?" she asked him.

"Yeah," he said as he helped her out of the Jeep. "Are you okay to do this?"

She nodded. He'd quickly gone over what she should expect. What questions they would ask her. What she would have to sign.

"We should be in and out in about an hour," he assured her.

Just over an hour later, they walked back out and climbed into his Jeep. She'd met all of his co-workers. His chief of police. His new partner. They had answered questions and signed documents. The entire process was quick and far less painful than she'd expected.

Even though it was only shortly after lunchtime, she realized she was mentally and physically exhausted.

"There's a good burger place on the corner next to my place. We can grab some burgers to go and take them to the beach?" he suggested.

"Sure," she said, resting her head back as he pulled out of the parking lot. She fell instantly asleep as he weaved through the busy streets of Miami. The sunshine hitting her through the windows helped dull her senses.

She woke when he ordered them burgers and asked for a shake as well. Then he parked at a two-story brick apartment building that sat directly next to an Indian restaurant.

"You live here?" she asked him.

"Yeah." He motioned with his full hands to the window he'd parked in front of. "That's my place. We can walk to the beach from here. It's just around the corner."

She reached over to take one of the food containers but he shifted them to his other hand and took her hand in his.

They walked for two blocks until they hit the beach. They sat in the sand and watched everyone enjoying themselves in the sun and surf while they ate.

She took a couple bites and instantly felt her stomach twist, so she set the food aside while Brock finished off his burger.

"Can't eat the rest?" he asked.

"No." She sighed. "It all makes me sick to my stomach. All of it." She turned to him. "My real name is Amber Oswald." She had been saying it in her head over and over since seeing it in print.

"And you have a twin," he pointed out.

"Yes," she said, looking down at her hand. Then she held it up and showed him one of the thin white scars on her fingers. "This is from one of the times I asked about Jade." She showed him her finger. "He almost cut it completely off." She looked at the scar then showed him another on her wrist. "This one is from when I thought about killing myself after he beat me because I'd asked about my mother. Thankfully, the blade was too dull."

She felt Brock tense beside her and then wrap his arm around her as tears rolled down her cheeks.

"That man put me through hell," she said, wiping the tears away. He held her as she cried. She didn't care if anyone stopped to stare at her or saw her crying. So much had been stripped from her so far, this was one area she just couldn't care about.

When her tears dried up, she opened her eyes and looked up at him. "I want him to pay."

"He will," he assured her. Just then his phone rang. "It's my dad." He answered the call. "Yeah, she's here."

"Hey, kiddo," Reggie said when Brock put the phone on speaker. "I know you've been through hell today. Kim and I just wanted you to know that we've got Emma for the night. She's having a blast swimming and enjoying herself. We've stuffed her with plenty of broccoli and other yucky vegetables and will deny anything she says to the contrary about chicken nuggets, ice cream and cookies," he added with a chuckle, causing Crissy to smile. Then he sobered slightly. "Take your time coming back tomorrow. I've got some good news. I've located your family. I've sent Brock a phone number. It's to their place in the Bahamas. When you feel like it, give them a call. I'd do it pretty quickly though, since news this big tends to get leaked to the press."

"Thanks," she said, her throat feeling raw.

"Any time," Reggie added. "Simon Jones is going to pay for this. The man will never walk free again. You have my word on that."

"Thank you." Crissy sighed.

"Take care of her, son," Reggie said before hanging up.

"Come on." Brock held out his hand. "Let's head back to my place."

She took his hand, and he helped her stand and pulled her instantly into his arms. "Amber," he said softly. "The name suits you." He pulled back and looked into her eyes.

She smiled. "Good, because... I don't want anything that will associate me with that man in my life again."

Brock nodded. "Amber it is from here on out."

She smiled. Then laughed. "Okay, it might take some getting used to."

Brock laughed and started walking. "When I was in third grade, some kids made fun of my name. They called me Broccoli the entire year." He smiled. "So the following year, I made all my friends start calling me by my middle name."

"Which is?"

"Ryan."

She stopped and looked at him. "Brock Ryan Miller." She nodded. "I like it."

"Yeah, so did a few of the kids. They started using it, only I never answered when they called out to me because it sounded foreign to me. Then the other kids started calling me Lion. Broccoli Lion." He rolled his eyes again. "I realized that no matter what I did, kids were going to be mean to me."

"What happened?" she asked as they reached his building.

"I gave up and learned to embrace my name," he answered. "I know it's not the same, but it may take some time for you to lose Crissy Talbot." He leaned in and kissed her just outside his door.

"Thanks," she said and smiled up at him. "Legally, I suppose I am both. Right? I mean, I do have a birth certificate with Crissy Jones, then a marriage license with Talbot."

"Yeah, we'll have to figure that one out later." He shut the door behind him. "For now, you look like you're about to fall over. How about a nap?"

"A nap sounds wonderful," she said with a sigh. "After I make a call."

Brock nodded. "Okay, let's do this together."

# CHAPTER SIXTEEN

Brock watched Crissy... Amber, struggle with dialing the phone number on his cell phone. She wiped her palms on her shorts several times before finally hitting the button.

They were sitting in his living room on his sofa, and he couldn't help but feeling as if the place no longer felt like home. It was dark and empty and more than anything he wanted to be back at the pool house with Emma and Amber, enjoying an evening swim.

She'd put the call on speaker, and he heard the phone ring twice before someone finally answered the call.

"Hello?" The woman's voice sounded soft. Too soft to make out much. But one thing was clear—the voice was almost identical to Crissy's. Amber's, he corrected in his head again.

"Hello, my name is Crissy..." She shook her head and took a deep breath. "Am I speaking with Jade Oswald?"

"Yes, this is Jade."

Brock took Amber's hand in his and squeezed it lightly.

"I... I'm sorry to bother you but... This may sound strange, but... I think I'm your twin." Amber looked over at him, and he nodded his encouragement.

The phone was silent for a moment, and he could see the worry in Amber's eyes. "Hello? Are you still there?" she asked.

"Yes, I'm here," Jade said softly. "Do you have a video app?"

"Yes, I..." Amber held the phone out and motioned to him to help her. "Brock, how do you connect a video call?"

Brock reached over and hit the button on the phone that would connect the video call for her.

The phone made a ringing sound and then was answered immediately.

On the screen popped up an image of a blond woman standing on a balcony with the blue ocean behind her.

It could have been Crissy—Amber—in a blond wig, and he sucked in his breath.

He felt Amber shake beside him and wrapped an arm around her shoulders.

They watched Jade's eyes pool up. "Amber?" she said just as a blond-haired, bare-chested man rushed to Jade's side and wrapped his arms around, her much like Brock was doing to Amber. "My god. It's really you," Jade cried out.

"Yes," Amber said with a nervous giggle. "I..."

"Where are you?" Jade asked quickly.

"Florida. Miami tonight. But I'm in Key West," Amber answered.

"Key West. So close." Jade sighed. "What... what happened? Where have you been?" Jade asked.

"That's a very long story." Amber sighed. "You're in the Bahamas?"

"Yes, my parents..." Jade smiled. "Our parents own a resort down here. We moved here a few years after you went missing. They thought it would be safer."

"The man who took me. He's in custody right now," Amber said.

"Did you just find out who you were?" Jade asked.

Amber nodded and looked over at him. "This is Brock. He helped me find out the truth."

"Hi." Jade smiled. "This is Wyatt. He's... well, it's complicated." Jade laughed.

"Hi." Amber smiled at the screen.

"Police?" Wyatt asked him.

Brock nodded and narrowed his eyes. "You?"

"Sort of," Wyatt said with a nod.

"Our parents?" Amber asked.

"They're in Europe right now. They are going to flip their lids." Jade laughed. "Oh my god! You're alive. You're right there." Jade pointed to the screen. "I love your hair! I've always wanted to chop my locks off."

"Don't you dare," Wyatt said in a low tone as he smiled.

Jade waved his comment away. Brock understood the moves and the subtle hints that they were a couple.

"I can come to the states..." Jade started but got a slight nudge from Wyatt and then added. "Soon. But right now... It's complicated." She frowned. "How about you? Can you travel here?"

Amber looked at him, and he could tell she was thinking of all the complications.

"I... need time to clear things up. Such as my passport." She laughed. "It has the wrong name on it."

"What name?" Jade asked.

"Crissy Talbot," Amber answered.

"Crissy... Talbot," Jade repeated.

"The girl who escaped the cop serial killers?" Wyatt asked.

"What?" Jade jerked to look at him.

"Yes," Amber said with a slight nod.

"You were kidnapped by a serial killer twenty-three years ago?" Jade asked.

"No, two years ago," Amber answered. "Like I said, it's complicated. The man that took me from you... raised me. Then, two years ago, I was kidnapped by... the other," Amber added.

"Oh my god," Jade said and the phone shook.

Brock leaned back and listened to the pair of them fill each other in on the basics of their lives. It was strange, seeing how similar they were. Even though Jade had long blond hair and did her makeup differently, they were identical even in the way they spoke.

"I have a niece?" Jade said cheerfully. "I can't wait to meet Emma."

"Soon," Amber promised.

When the sisters hung up, he pulled her down against his chest.

"Can you shut down for a while?" he asked her.

"Yes, as exciting as that all was, I'm oddly beat." She laughed when he lifted her off the sofa and carried her into his room.

As they settled on the bed, wrapped around one another, he whispered next to her ear, "Later, I'm going to want to enjoy you in my bed." Then he fell asleep.

He was slightly disoriented when he woke up. For a split second, with the smell of Crissy surrounding him, he believed he was back in the Keys. Then he remembered everything and automatically corrected his thinking. Amber, he told himself. She was Amber.

He knew how important it was to her to move forward. To retake what had been stolen from her so long ago.

Much like he was sure that sex with him was her taking back the pleasure of the act that had been stolen from her as well. He just hoped that it meant as much to her as it did to him.

He shifted her closer and just enjoyed the feel and scent of her. He didn't care which name she wanted to go by—it was the essence of her that he desired.

She was an incredible mother and woman no matter what name she went by. The more he lay there and listened to her soft breathing, feeling her body against his, the more he realized what kind of future he wanted.

His tiny apartment felt empty. Useless. The noise from the city outside his window was more annoying than ever before. He wanted the slow pace of the Keys. The lazy life with Amber and Emma.

He knew what he had to do and knew just the man who could make it happen.

With his mind made up, he shifted slightly as Amber woke up.

"Hey," he said softly, brushing a strand of her short dark hair away from her face.

"Hey." She smiled back at him. "How long were we out?"

"Long enough." He kissed her. She rolled over on top of him and, just being with her like this, he felt more at home than he had since returning to Miami.

After showering and changing, they walked hand in hand down to a little taco bar on the beach that he liked and had dinner.

He hadn't thought anything of it, but as they were sitting there, a news report flashed on the massive television screen above the bar. Suddenly, Amber's face filled the screen.

"Shocking news in the Miami brothers serial killer case. It has been leaked that the true identity of the sole survivor in that heinous crime, Crissy Talbot, is Amber Oswald, solving a case that is two decades old. Amber was only four when she was kidnapped by Simon Jones, a criminal with a long rap sheet, including multiple DUIs and theft, who, after a failed attempt at ransom, raised the young girl as his own daughter and hid her away for years. The Oswalds, a prominent family with ties to the White House, have yet to return our calls for comment."

He turned to Amber. "Are you okay?" he asked her softly as several eyes moved in their direction and whispers turned into loud chatter around them.

"I think it's time we left," she replied.

"Yeah." He tossed some money down on the table and took her hand. Amber stopped him and stared up at the screen as another report started.

"In other news, another body was discovered in the recent copy-cat case of those serial killers. The first victim was a fifteen-year-old runaway discovered in an abandoned warehouse. Earlier this morning, our very own Rebecca Clint was on the scene at another warehouse where the body of Sara Gibbons, a seventeen-year-old that went missing last week, was discovered."

Amber's hand tightened in his. He pulled her away from the report and out into the street just as her panic attack hit her full force.

He heard several people shouting at them and knew that they were being recorded and photographed as he lifted Amber up into his arms and raced back to his apartment with a crowd of people in tow.

"Breathe," he said once they were safely inside. He set her down and held her head between her knees as she gasped for air.

"I... can't..." She shook her head.

"Yes, you can," he said softly. "In one, out two." He repeated the counting until her breathing slowed.

"Did you know?" she asked him.

"No." He shook his head. "I think we were too busy with Simon this morning. I had a few missed calls. My dad probably figured we'd dealt with enough for today."

She sat back and nodded her head. "I want to go home," she said. "I know we planned on staying, but... I need my baby."

He smiled and wrapped his arms around her. "I'll get our things."

"Brock?" she said when he stood up to gather their bags.

"Yeah?"

"Thank you for understanding," she said, looking down at her hands.

He walked over and took her hands in his, then pulled her to her feet and held onto her. "Always," he said into her hair.

They waited until the crowd died down outside of his apartment. When there were only a few stragglers outside, they rushed to the Jeep and drove away as quickly as possible.

The drive back to the Keys was quiet. He'd called his parents, and they suggested they come stay the night at their place since Emma was already fast asleep.

When they arrived, Amber crawled in bed with her

daughter, and he sat up with his dad and was filled in on both cases.

Rebecca Clint's body was discovered by a cleaning crew. The building she was found in was under construction, not abandoned.

"There were construction cameras everywhere," his father said with a slight nod. "We have him." He showed him the photos on his phone. "There's a statewide manhunt right now."

"Why wasn't this on the news?" he asked, looking at the grainy image.

"We don't want to spook him into doing something drastic," his dad answered. "For now, go on up, get some rest." He nodded to the stairs. "Be with your family."

Brock paused and then smiled. "They are that, aren't they?"

His dad laughed. "Son, that woman and child already know that you love them. Just make sure to tell them. Soon."

He stood up and hugged his father and then did what he suggested. He crawled in bed with the two girls that he loved.

He woke to the smell of freshly baked cinnamon rolls and realized that the bed was empty. Crawling out, he showered, dressed, and walked into the kitchen just as Amber set a large pan of rolls on the countertop.

"There he is. Amber was just telling us how much you love these," his mother said cheerfully. He liked that his parents had gotten on board immediately with calling her Amber instead of Crissy. It was just one more reason to love them.

"Morning." He walked over and kissed his mother on the cheek, then did the same to Amber.

"Me too," Emma called out from her chair at the table.

Laughing, he walked over and picked her up and rained kisses over her cheek as she giggled.

"Did you miss us?" he asked Emma.

"So much." Emma giggled. "Grandma Kimmy let me have cookies and ice cream."

He smiled over at his mother. "Did she? Did you eat a whole lot of cookies?"

"No." Emma giggled. "I only had one." She held up her little finger. "I wanted four." She switched her fingers and, after some effort, finally held up four fingers. "I'm gonna be three soon."

He smiled at the tiny digit, then kissed her again. "I know." He smiled and sat next to her. "What kinds of presents do you want?"

"Books!" Emma cheered loudly, causing everyone to laugh.

"I have a box of books that are too young for Ellie and Celia upstairs. They're probably just right for you though, Emma," his mother said as she set a plate of cinnamon rolls on the table.

Just then his father stepped into the room, and instantly Brock knew something was wrong.

"What?" he asked, breaking into the happy conversation.

"It's nothing," his father said cheerfully. "Amber and Brock, let's step outside for a moment."

Amber dried her hands on a hand towel and then followed him and his father outside on the back deck.

Brock wrapped his arms around Amber and held on.

"Your ex-husband broke into your place early this morning shortly after you two arrived here," his father said clearly.

Brock felt Amber's knees go weak and reached over to hold onto her. "What?" she asked.

"We have him in custody. It appears that the news report telling the world that you're from a very wealthy family set him off. He believes you've known this for years and is demanding his fair share of your family's riches," his father finished.

Amber groaned. "Shit."

"He was high or drunk off his rocker. We're not sure how he got down here since there was no car..." His father shook his head.

"His license was taken away last year," Amber said. "Most likely his latest fling drove him. If we're lucky, she abandoned him here," Amber said, walking over to lean on the railing.

"Those security cameras you hung up did the trick. He barely made it in the front door, which, by the way, needs to be replaced. He shattered it before we were on him. Until it can be replaced, why don't the three of you plan on staying here."

He looked towards Amber, who nodded her head slightly. "Thank you," she said.

His father slapped him on the shoulder. "I'll arrange for the door to be fixed. Your mom's been wanting to add a few updates to the place anyway," he said before walking inside.

Brock wrapped his arms around Amber as they looked out over the water.

"Things are going to get complicated now. Aren't they?" she said with a sigh.

"They don't have to be. You've already won the battle with him once. With this against him, no judge would allow him near that little girl," he said confidently.

"You're right." Amber nodded. "I know you're right."

He turned her in his arms and kissed her. "I was going to tell you later, but..." He searched her eyes and felt that it was the right time. "I love you. I love both of you. I want to be in your lives. If you'll have me."

Amber smiled up at him, and he felt her arms tighten around him. "Yes," she said, and he watched tears fill her eyes. "Yes, we'd like that too." She nodded and then lifted on her toes and kissed him. "We love you too."

## CHAPTER SEVENTEEN

Thanks to Brock's parents, she was getting used to her new name. Well, her original name. Kim made a point to use it often and even had Emma dancing around singing a silly tune using it, which was very catchy and annoying at the same time.

They had arranged for the front door on the pool house to be replaced since eighty percent of it had been stained glass and was now, apparently, in pieces. She wanted to pay for the damages Carl had caused, but neither of them would hear of it and mentioned that the costs would be covered by their insurance.

They'd also hired a service to go in and clean the rental so she could have the week off. Kim had arranged for a few upgrades in the pool house. New security systems were being put in as well as some high-tech internet service and cable television. Even if she wasn't going to use it, Kim wanted it there just in case. Even the pool was getting cleaned by a service while she was away.

She knew that it was at a great cost to the Millers and

tried to object. She couldn't really afford to take time off, as she was trying to save up for Emma's birthday gift, but they insisted that she would be paid for the time anyway. Kim claimed that since they were having all the carpets professional cleaned and the place was being fumigated for termites, that she and Emma would have had to be out of the building anyway.

She knew what the Millers were doing and figured that she'd enjoy their kindness for now. After all, there was a lot she could do to repay them in the future.

For the next two days, she and Emma enjoyed their time off and time with Brock's family. They even spent a fun day at the beach.

They received an email update from Judge Reeves, who, after being assigned Carl's case against Amber, and hearing about Carl's arrest, threw his new case out completely.

She was getting so used to her new identity that she even thought of herself as Amber Oswald in her sleep.

They ran into Beth and Tilly the last night they were going to be staying with the Millers. They had all piled in the car and driven to Key West to eat at Oscar's.

"Amber." Beth rushed to her and hugged her, shifting Johnathan in her arms to do so. "I saw the news." Her friend smiled at her. "How are you doing?"

She smiled. "Better. Thanks for calling me Amber." She tickled Johnathan's cheek. The little boy giggled and held onto her finger.

Instantly, she wished for another child and her eyes landed on Brock, who was talking to a few locals while he held Emma in his arms. Maybe a boy this time. One that looked like Brock, she thought with a smile.

"The name suits you. So does whatever is making you

look so relaxed and happy." Beth waved her fingers over Amber's face, then leaned closer and whispered. "Must be all thanks to Brock." She nodded to where he stood laughing.

"It is," she admitted. "And the mini vacation we're having. Which ends tomorrow," she added with a slight groan.

"There's been a slew of workers coming and going at the rental in the past two days. I heard about the break-in. I'm so happy your ex is rotting in a cell," Beth added.

"No one would pay his bail," she said with a smile. "Maybe it'll give him a chance to sober up. To be honest, he wasn't such a bad guy when I first met him."

"That's what drugs will do to you," Beth added. "I remember all my dad went through before he sobered up."

"What are you guys doing here tonight?" Amber asked.

"Celebrating. Oscar's won best restaurant in the Keys again this year." In a quieter voice, she said, "That tidbit of news won't be released until next week, but we know." She winked at her. "Go on." Beth waved at her. "Go sit and enjoy with your family," she said as the Miller's name was called for their table.

Brock was carrying Emma and sat her down next to him and started coloring with her while she chatted with his parents.

Kim was filling her in on a few improvements they'd made with the rental and the pool house. She couldn't wait to get back there to see all the neat things she had described.

She ordered Oscar's special for the night, as did Brock and Reggie. The fish plate was so delicious, she gobbled it up while Brock helped Emma eat her chicken nuggets and macaroni and cheese.

She was roughly halfway through her dinner when her

stomach started acting up and her head started spinning. She quietly excused herself and immediately went into the bathroom and got sick. Her palms felt clammy, and her head was spinning. She felt as if she was on the verge of passing out and stumbled from the bathroom, desperate to get to Brock for help.

She didn't even have time to react when strong arms wrapped around her and pulled her into the darkness.

She didn't know how much time had passed when she finally woke. Her entire body ached, and she once again emptied the contents of her stomach.

"Well, well, well. Lookie who's awake early. Oh, don't worry about getting sick, sweetie, that's just the drugs wearing off." The moment she heard the voice, she remembered it. Remembered the pain and suffering that had come next. Her entire body jerked as the urge to flee overcame her. Only she came up short when her hands and legs wouldn't move.

Tears had blinded her, and she desperately blinked several times to clear her vision.

Standing over her was a teenage boy wearing black pants and a white button-up shirt. He looked like... a waiter.

His sandy-blond hair was short, neatly cut. He looked like the all-American kid. Good-looking but not so good-looking as to get too much attention.

Wherever they were, it was too dark to see much. A thin beam of light was coming from a few feet away, casting just enough light on them so she could see her captor's expression of glee.

"There she is." He smiled down at her and then moved closer. "Imagine my luck," he said, leaning down in front of her. "I'd been wondering how to get to you at that fancy mansion you've been staying at. I knew after watching Carl get snatched that it wasn't safe to get to you there. Too many damned cameras." He shook his head and made a soft tsking noise. "They've been installing even more over the past few days. I was lucky enough to follow that old rich bitch back to where you were staying now." He smiled. "That place is a fucking fortress. I had to rent a boat just to get a view of it, but even the waters are patrolled around the whole damned island. I tried a few times to trick the guards into letting me through the gates, but no luck." He shook his head again. "I guess my diligence in sitting and waiting finally paid off tonight when I saw y'all head out and followed you here. I only had to kill one waiter out on a smoke break for these." He motioned to his shirt. "Still, they're a pretty good fit." He laughed. "And I enjoyed the kill."

She threw up again, this time not turning her head away, so she hit him straight in the face with her bile.

He jerked back and yelled, "You bitch." Then he fisted his hand and plowed it into the side of her face. Once again, everything went dark.

This time when she woke, it was clear she was in the trunk of a car traveling at high speed. He was taking her away from her family. Away from Emma and Brock.

She fought the restraints on her hands. After last time, she'd studied all the ways to break free from restraints. She was surprised at how quickly and easily they came undone. Since it was too dark to see, she tried to figure out if he'd done that by design or if she'd just gotten lucky.

He'd used zip ties. Thin ones. Could he have really been that careless and stupid? She reached down and struggled a little more with the one's wrapped around her bare ankles.

She'd worn a simple cotton sundress for the evening dinner and her favorite sandals. She instantly regretted leaving her purse hanging on her chair at the dinner table when she'd rushed to the bathroom. She doubted he'd be dumb enough to bring it with her, but still... She could have... what? Used the pepper spray in it? She hadn't even fought him off when he'd snagged her. No, she'd just passed out right in his waiting arms.

What had he said? He'd drugged her. Her mind snapped suddenly. It was as if the veil had been lifted. He'd drugged her, which meant he had been their waiter. She remembered him now, serving them all food. When they'd arrived, a dark-haired man had taken their drink orders and delivered her glass of wine. But it had been this guy, the blond-haired one, who had delivered their meals. Oh god. He'd killed their waiter and drugged her dinner.

Had he drugged Brock's and Reggie's dinners as well? What about Emma? She tensed at that thought.

How was she going to get out of there? Where was he taking her?

She remembered how Emily and Jamie had escaped the trunk of Daryl Collins's patrol car. How he'd busted off the emergency latch handle, but Jamie had used her high heels and forced the lid of the trunk open. Then she'd shoved Emily out onto the road while she'd waited and fought with Collins until help had arrived, all thanks to the tracking device Blaine had given her in a necklace.

She didn't have such a device. She wasn't even wearing jewelry. Brock wouldn't be coming for her. He had no clue where she was. Did he even know that she was gone?

She fought back the tears once more and took several cleansing breaths. She was not going to become a victim again, she told herself. She was Amber Oswald not Crissy Talbot.

Searching around with her hands, she found some trash and a duffle bag. Inside the bag was some duct tape and papers. She searched for the trunk's emergency release but didn't find any latches.

The car jerked as if it had turned off the highway, but then sped up again. Then loud music started playing, and she could hear him singing along with it.

Her attention turned to the front of the trunk where a beam of light shown through the split back seats. She scooted closer and peeked through the slats.

She could see him singing along to the song, tapping the steering wheel as if he was having the time of his life. She laid her hand on the back of the seat and was surprised when it fell forward, leaving half of the trunk now exposed to the front of the car. Since the music was so loud, he hadn't even heard a thing.

Scooting her upper body forward, she searched the floorboard of the back seat. Here, she found a heavy tire iron and a thick rope.

She thought about hitting him over the head with the tire iron, but could she muster up enough strength to knock him out? What would happen to her if she didn't? He could snatch it from her and use it on her?

Then she thought about the rope and realized that was the only way to ensure she stayed in control.

Slowly and as quietly as she could, she pulled her legs out of the trunk, squatted, and positioned herself directly behind the driver seat. She made sure to stay out of the range of the rearview mirror. Wrapping the ropes around her hands, she waited until she felt the car slow down before she made her move.

With thoughts of seeing her daughter and Brock again, she used all her strength to shove the rope over his head and around his neck and the headrest. She leaned back as far as she could against the ropes, cutting off his air.

The car jerked forward as his foot jammed on the brakes while his hands left the steering wheel, letting the car jerk off the road towards the ditch.

She wanted to scream and grab the wheel, but she held fast and braced herself as best as she could for the crash. Only, it didn't come. Instead, the car continued into the tall grass and even sped up when his foot jammed on the gas pedal while he desperately tried to reach around and free himself.

She braced her knees against the back of the seat, leaning far back out of his reach while the rope tightened around his neck. She wasn't going to allow him to touch her. Not again.

She didn't know how long the car continued to drive through the dark field of grass or how long she fought to hold the rope around his neck.

When the car started to slow and he began to stop fighting, she still held fast, putting all of her weight on the rope, even as it bit into the skin on her palms. Blood oozed out of her skin and the joints and bones in her fingers ached and cried to be released from the pressure.

Only after the car came to a complete stop and the man stopped fighting did she let up on the rope a little. She hovered there for a few moments, scared that he'd jerk awake and she'd lose once more.

The music on the radio was still blaring so loudly that she couldn't hear if he was breathing. Deciding not to chance it, she let the rope slip to his chest. She wrapped it a couple times around his chest and tied it tightly in a knot.

Leaning forward, she reached up and shut off the music. The silence caused her head to spin. Her ears rang, as if missing the noise. She waited several heartbeats, never once taking her eyes off of the man, before searching the car for a cell phone.

She found one along with a gun in the glove box.

When she dialed 911, she felt some sense of relief upon hearing the operator's voice. But then everything burst out of her, and she was barely able to get a legible word out.

After spewing what had happened to her, her name, both of them, Crissy Talbot and Amber Oswald, she explained that she didn't know where she was. Didn't know how far he'd driven her.

Seeing the clock on the dash, she realized it had been roughly an hour since she and the Millers had been seated at Oscar's.

She held onto the phone tightly as she continued to talk back and forth with the dispatcher, clinging desperately to the hope that they would find her soon.

Almost fifteen minutes later, she could hear the sirens of a police cruiser that had been sent out looking for her.

The operator had explained that, since she hadn't been gone that long, she was probably still in the Lower Keys somewhere. They were having the local PD drive around some of the most remote parts of the Keys with their sirens on. When she heard it, she cried and told the operator, who told all the cruisers to stop where they were.

Taking the phone with her, she climbed out of the car, not even glancing back at the man still tied to the seat, and began following the tire tracks through the tall grass in the field until she reached the road.

When she saw the lights, she screamed out and rushed towards them, waving her hands. A female officer ran towards her, and she didn't stop until she had her arms wrapped around the woman. Then her knees buckled out from under her as they both fell to the ground.

"You're okay, sweetie," the officer said calmly. "I've got you. You did good."

## CHAPTER EIGHTEEN

Brock woke with pins and needles rushing through his entire body.

"Easy son," his father said calmly.

Brock saw his face hovering over him.

"We're at the hospital. They've pumped your stomach," his father said. "They just finished up with you and are about to get to me." He groaned and turned a little paler.

"What happened?" he asked, then jerked up. "Emma?"

"She's fine," his father added. "So far she and your mother don't appear to have been affected. Nor anyone else in the place."

"Amber?" he asked, lying back down on the hospital bed, feeling queasy.

When his question was met with silence, he glanced over at his father, who was looking at him strangely.

"We think he poisoned us to snag her," his father said.

"What?" He jerked up and, before his father could stop him, he stood up and started rushing out of the small room.

His father rushed after him as Brock willed the sickness and spinning away.

He had to grab hold of the nurse's desk to not hit the floor.

"They're out looking for her," his father said. "We'll get her."

"Where's Emma?" he asked.

"She's with your mother." His father looked a little pale as he grabbed his stomach. "Damn it," he said before racing towards a trash can and throwing up.

Two nurses rushed over and took his arms to steady him.

"I'm okay," his father said as several police officers rushed through the emergency doors.

"Where are we at?" he demanded from them.

They looked past him to his father, who waved his hand. "Brock is in charge until I'm over this."

Brock turned back to the officers and asked again, "Where are we at?"

The older female officer stepped forward and nodded. "Sir, Officer Alice Brigs," she said quickly. "We've discovered the body of Mike Rowlett in the alley behind Oscar's. It appears Rowlett was out on a smoke break, waiting for your table's orders to come up, when he was jumped. He was hit over the head with something sharp, most likely a tire iron from the looks of it. Killed him in one blow. He was stripped clean. We suspect whoever poisoned your table took his place and delivered your meals."

"How did he get Amber out of the restaurant?" he asked Brigs.

"It appears he snuck her out the door at the end of the hallway. The woman's restroom is closest to that back door. If she was as incapacitated as the two of you were"—she motioned to him and his father, who was being shoved back onto a gurney and carted away again while he was vomiting into a bucket— "she probably couldn't put up much of a fight."

Just then their radio's squawked, and Officer Brigs leaned closer to listen.

"We've got her, sir," she said. "She's on with a dispatcher claiming she's incapacitated her perp and doesn't know where she is. The dispatcher has requested we do a ground search with our sirens and lights on. She thinks she might still be in the Lower Keys."

"How long..." He glanced at his watch. "Twenty-five minutes," he answered himself, "since she left to go to the bathroom." He raced towards the door. "I'm with you Brigs," he said as he exited the building.

"Yes, sir," Brigs said, rushing beside him.

"Twenty-five minutes. Five at most to load her up and head out," he said as he thought out loud. He turned to the officer. "Ask the dispatcher to ask her what's around her."

He climbed in the passenger seat as Brigs started the patrol car and asked the question.

"Fields and grass," Brigs responded after getting the answer.

"She could be on one of the Sugarloaf Keys or Cudjoe. Get all your patrols out there and drive along any rural areas with lights and sirens blaring. Just in case, send patrols to Summerland and Ramrod. I doubt he got that far."

They had just made it to Shark Key Bridge when a female officer got on the radio.

"10-65 in custody, possible 10-54." He felt his body tense. 10-54. Possible dead body. "County road 939, mile marker..." There was a pause. "Three."

He turned to Brigs. "Get me there in two minutes." He grabbed the radio.

"Yes, sir," Brigs said, and he felt the car lurch forward as he requested more information from the officer.

Instead of her responding, Amber's voice replied.

"Brock?" She sounded hysterical.

"Baby," he said over the radio. "My god. Are you okay?"

"Yes," she replied back quickly. "Emma?"

"She's safe and with my mother. I'm on the way to you now. Use the officer's phone and call me on my cell, so we can get off the official channel."

His phone rang seconds later. Happily, he answered the video call.

Amber's face filled the screen and when she saw him, she burst into tears.

"I think I killed him," she cried.

He tensed. "Is the officer there?" he asked. Suddenly the phone shifted, and a female officer's face came into view, one that he knew very well. "Officer Meyers, have you checked yet?" he asked.

"No, sir. I felt it best to stay with Amber here," she answered easily. Then she glanced up. "Backup is here. I'll give you back to Amber." Meyers handed the phone over, and Amber's face once more filled the screen.

"We're still a few minutes out," he told her. "Did he hurt you?" he asked, running his eyes over her.

She turned her head slightly and he saw a trickle of blood on her left temple.

"He hit me with his fist. Knocked me out. He said he poisoned me," Amber said.

"Yeah, he got me and my dad too," he told her as the patrol car turned off the main highway and onto 939. "Three miles away from you," he told her. "I'm never going to let you go again."

"Okay." She smiled at him as tears rolled down her cheeks.

He could see the lights of the two patrol cars up ahead and, as Brigs pulled up behind one, he jumped out and met Amber's waiting arms.

"I'm here," he said over and over again. "I'm right here. I've got you." He kissed her cheek as she cried.

Over her head, he watched two officers appear from the bushes, carting a body. He was slightly surprised when the man jerked his head up.

"You didn't kill him," he said to Amber. "See, he's still alive. He'll pay for what he did for the rest of his life."

She jerked her head around, and they both watched the two officers strong-arm the guy into the back of a patrol car.

"He's just a kid," Amber said. "He can't be more than eighteen."

"Then he'll have a very long time behind bars." He walked her back to Brig's patrol car to wait for an ambulance to take him and Amber back to the hospital. He hated to admit it, but he was weaker than he'd expected.

Almost two hours later, they sat in his father's hospital room, listening to the monitors as they filled his dad in. His father had ingested more of the drug than he had. They had yet to identify it since there were more than a dozen different pill bottles in the back seat of the sedan, along with the tire iron that they suspected had killed Mike Rowlett.

Amber sat in the chair, holding Emma as her daughter slept in her arms. She had been thoroughly checked out by doctors and medically cleared. She had the tiniest bandage on her temple. White bandages covered the rope burns on both of her hands.

Since the man who had kidnapped her wasn't completely coherent and there wasn't any identification in the stolen car, they were waiting for the fingerprints to come back in order to identify him.

Amber had done a number on him. The guy, suspected to be in his late teens, was still having difficulty breathing and talking and was slipping in and out of consciousness.

His father was complaining that he couldn't oversee the investigation but was thankful Brock had taken the reins.

"I knew you had it in you," his father said softly.

"What? Bossing people around to find the love of my life?" Brock responded with a slight wink to Amber, who smiled back at him.

"Yeah," his dad joked. "Which is why, after this, I'm ready to retire and appoint you chief of police. Of course, there's some red tape we'll have to go through first, but after today, I think everyone will be on board with my decision."

"Dad," he started to say but stopped. How many years had his dad egged him to take the job? For so long, he'd turned it down because it didn't suit him. Now, however, he couldn't think of anything better. "Thanks," he finished with a smile.

"Sure thing." His dad sighed. "Now, since I have to spend the rest of the night here being checked out, why don't you take your family home?" He motioned to Amber and Emma. "Get some rest. I'm sure there will be more answers in the morning."

He gently took Emma from Amber's arms and then walked hand in hand with her out of the hospital. Since his Jeep was still at his parents' place, they hitched a ride with Officer Myers back to their place. Amber wanted Emma to be able to wake up in her own bed.

When they stepped into the house, Amber followed him as he carried Emma up the stairs.

"Here," she said, turning on a low light. "Let's get her in some pajamas." She stopped. "What?"

He turned to where Amber was looking. There, on the left side of Emma's bedroom, was a brand-new bookshelf that filled the entire wall. He smiled when he saw it was completely full of books.

"I'd say my mother's birthday gift to Emma came a little early," he said softly. "She's going to love this when she wakes up."

Amber stood there, her bandaged hands over her mouth as her eyes teared up.

Leaving Emma asleep and fully dressed on the bed, he walked over and wrapped his arms around her.

"You're okay," he said to her again. "She's okay. We're okay." He rocked her slowly in his arms.

"I know," she said softly. "I now have something I've always wanted." She pulled back and smiled up at him. "A family." She kissed him.

He looked down at her and felt his heart swell at the thought of a future with her.

Then he stepped back, bent down, and held her hand in his. "I don't have a ring. I should, but I don't. We can get one together. The three of us." He shook his head, feeling suddenly very stupid. He should have thought of what to say. He should have planned this better. "I should have planned this better," he said, kicking himself and causing Amber to smile.

"You're doing fine. Go on," she encouraged him.

He cleared his throat. "Okay." He took a deep breath. "Amber..." He frowned. "I don't even know your middle name."

She laughed. "Neither do I. I forgot to ask."

He nodded. "Amber, middle name to be filled in later,

Oswald, I want to make a new life with you. Here, in the Keys. With you and with Emma. Will you marry me?"

She smiled and then tugged on his hands until he stood up next to her. "Yes, I will."

"Does this mean I have a daddy now?" Emma's voice had them both turning.

"Yes," Amber laughed. "It does."

Answers did come in the following day. Loads of them.

First off, Corey John Willingham, aka CJ Willy, had first been arrested at the tender age of thirteen. The arresting officer was none other than Daryl Collins, who not only bailed CJ out several more times that year but had seemingly taken him under his wing.

It was reported that CJ, having no family of his own, had been in and out of foster homes until the time that Collins and Alcott took him in.

They had even matched DNA left in the shipping container with CJ's. Even though the kid liked to use condoms on his victims, there was enough there to prosecute him for a few more murders besides the recent ones.

The stolen car supplied enough evidence to put CJ away for life. There was obvious evidence of the murders of the two women, including video of the heinous acts. There were several more videos of women they had yet to find. Four more to be exact.

CJ explained how he targeted runaways. It was easy to lure them away since they had that in common.

They were matching the duct tape found in the back seat and the rope with fibers left on both of those bodies. He liked to burn his victims. Enjoyed the smell of burning flesh. He even talked on one of the videos about how wonderful it tasted. The kid was a complete psychopath. Just like Collins and Alcott had been.

The tire iron in the back seat was in fact the murder weapon used to kill Mike Rowlett, a twenty-year-old student who had just been hired on at Oscar's for the summer months.

Of course, the news of the third serial killer's capture was on every channel. As was Amber's involvement.

There was a group of television vans parked in front of the rental. Thankfully, his mother had had the forethought to cancel the next reservations so that Amber didn't have to deal with work. Nor did guests have to deal with the crazy media camping out on the street and shouting questions at them as they tried to vacation.

It was just past supper time when there was a knock on the front door. His father had stationed two officers on the street, so he immediately knew whoever it was had passed security scrutiny.

Walking over, he opened the door to a couple roughly his parents' age.

"Hi," the man said and glanced at him. "Are you Brock Miller?"

"Yes," Brock answered and before they even said anything else, he knew who they were. Amber was a spitting image of the woman standing in front of him.

"We're Patrick and Julia Oswald." The man held out his hand for Brock.

Brock felt his heart skip. "Of course." He motioned for them to come in.

"Amber?" Julia called out and rushed forward.

"Mom?" Amber cried out when she saw the woman. Setting Emma down, she rushed across the room and held onto the woman as they both cried.

"I guess this confirms it," Patrick said beside him. "We had our doubts." He shook his head. "Damned if she doesn't look exactly like Jade." He glanced over at him.

"Except the hair," Brock added and Patrick laughed.

"Dad?" Amber held out a hand and Brock watched the man step forward and engulf the two women.

Brock walked over and lifted Emma into his arms easily.

"Who?" Emma asked softly.

"I hear I have a grandchild," Julia said suddenly as she stepped back when she heard Emma talk. Then she walked over and took Emma's hand in hers. "I'm your grandmother," Julia added as she wiped her tears away with her free hand.

"I have two grandmothers?" Emma asked him excitedly.

"And two grandfathers," Patrick added as he held onto Amber and looked at Emma.

"These are my parents," Brock said, shifting Emma into Julia's waiting arms. "Reggie and Kimberly Miller." He motioned to his parents who had been sitting on the sofa, watching, and now stood up to shake hands with the other couple.

After a brief greeting, they all sat around and filled her parents in as best as they could.

"What's my name?" Amber asked suddenly. "My full name?"

Her mother smiled at her. "Amber Emma Oswald," her mother answered, nodding to Emma. "You must have clung on to something from your past."

"I... remembered Jade too," she said. "I always believed she was made up."

"She can't wait to see you. Unfortunately, she had some... business before she could come up here." Her mother glanced at her father.

"We were going to head down there and see her," Amber said, taking Brock's hand in hers. "We could use the vacation."

"After we heal and let things settle down," Brock added.

"Where are you staying?" his mother asked suddenly.

"We normally have a steady rental here in the Keys, but it was completely booked up," Julia answered.

His mother smiled and winked at Amber.

"We've got a perfect place for you." She nodded towards the glass doors. "And I hear that the manager of the property is soon to be my daughter-in-law."

Brock watched happiness cross the couple's faces. They moved in for another hug, when Patrick's phone rang. The man, smiling, answered the call. Instantly, his smile disappeared as he listened. Then worry flashed in his eyes.

"I understand. We're on our way." He said, glancing around the room as if trying to gather his thoughts.

"What is it?" When he hung up, Julia asked.

"Jade's missing." Patrick said, taking his wife's hand. "Wyatt thinks she's been kidnapped."

"Let's go." Amber said, taking Emma back into her arms and looking at him. "My sister needs me."

He nodded. "Let's go to the Bahamas."

# ALSO BY JILL SANDERS

**The Pride Series**

Finding Pride

Discovering Pride

Returning Pride

Lasting Pride

Serving Pride

Red Hot Christmas

My Sweet Valentine

Return To Me

Rescue Me

A Pride Christmas

**The Secret Series**

Secret Seduction

Secret Pleasure

Secret Guardian

Secret Passions

Secret Identity

Secret Sauce

Secret Obsession

Secret Desire

Secret Charm

## The West Series

Loving Lauren

Taming Alex

Holding Haley

Missy's Moment

Breaking Travis

Roping Ryan

Wild Bride

Corey's Catch

Tessa's Turn

Saving Trace

Christmas Holly

## The Grayton Series

Last Resort

Someday Beach

Rip Current

In Too Deep

Swept Away

High Tide

Sunset Dreams

## Lucky Series

Unlucky In Love

Sweet Resolve

Best of Luck

A Little Luck

Christmas Wish

**Silver Cove Series**

Silver Lining

French Kiss

Happy Accident

Hidden Charm

A Silver Cove Christmas

Sweet Surrender

Second Chances

**Entangled Series – Paranormal Romance**

The Awakening

The Beckoning

The Ascension

The Presence

The Calling

The Chosen

**Haven, Montana Series**

Closer to You

Never Let Go

Holding On

Coming Home

The Hard Way

**Pride Oregon Series**

A Dash of Love

My Kind of Love

Season of Love

Tis the Season

Dare to Love

Where I Belong

Because of Love

A Thing Called Love

First Comes Love

Someone to Love

**Wildflowers Series**

Summer Nights

Summer Heat

Summer Secrets

Summer Fling

Summer's End

Summer's Wish

**Distracted Series**

Wake Me

Tame Me

Save Me

Dare Me

**Stand Alone Books**

Twisted Rock

Hope Harbor

Raven Falls

Angel Bluff

For a complete list of books:

http://JillSanders.com

# ABOUT THE AUTHOR

*Jill Sanders is a New York Times, USA Today, and international bestselling author of Sweet Contemporary Romance, Romantic Suspense, Western Romance, and Paranormal Romance novels. With over 75 books in eleven series, translations into several different languages, and audiobooks there's plenty to choose from. Look for Jill's bestselling stories wherever romance books are sold or visit her at jillsanders.com*

*Jill comes from a large family with six siblings, including an identical twin. She was raised in the Pacific Northwest and later relocated to Colorado for college and a successful IT career before discovering her talent for writing sweet and sexy page-turners. After Colorado, she decided to move south, living in Texas and now making her home along the Emerald Coast of Florida. You will find that the settings of several of her series are inspired by her time spent living in these areas. She has two sons and off-set the testosterone in her house by adopting three furry little ladies that provide her company while she's locked in her writing cave. She enjoys heading to the beach, hiking, swimming, wine-tasting, and pickleball with her husband, and of course writing. If you have read any of her books, you may also notice that there is a love of food, especially sweets! She has been blamed for a few added pounds by her assistant, editor, and fans... donuts or pie anyone?*

facebook.com/JillSandersBooks

twitter.com/JillMSanders

amazon.com/Jill-Sanders/e/B009M2NFD6?tag=jillm-com-20

bookbub.com/authors/jill-sanders

instagram.com/jillsandersauthor